EXPLICIT
EROTIC SEX STORIES

I Said Yes: Liv's Fantasy Comes True –
Hot and Steamy Threesome Erotic Story

By **Julia Saint**

Life can be tricky. It may take a person a while before they realize how much truth is in that statement. It's funny how life never seems to go quite the way you expect it to.

I thought I had my life carefully planned. I was what was referred to as a good girl. I attended an Ivy League University, graduated with honors, and by all accounts, was doing rather well. My first job was with a major magazine, working as a freelance writer. It had it's perks. I made good money, set my own hours, and made some great friendships along the way. Most people would have said I had a good life and things had fallen in track with my plans.

That would have all been true until recently but things change in a moments notice. Sometimes, you have less than a minute to make a choice and sometimes, a single choice can change the course of events beyond your wildest imagination.

My imagination can definitely be described as a bit wild. For example, I had a rather creative dream that, over time, developed into what I would label a fantasy. I actually looked up the meaning of fantasy to be sure it fit the situation. The definition included the following: imagining things that are impossible or improbable. In general, that would mean, it's simply not going to happen. At least one would think that's what it implied. However, I shared my rather creative dream with Brian, one of my best friends and my lover.

Who knew sharing an intimate moment and a few fanciful subconscious thoughts would change my life in so many interesting ways. Umm, not me, that's for sure. And no one in their right mind, or at least no one who knew me, would have ever thought that I would find myself in a situation like the one I found myself in shortly after talking with Brian.

How rare is it for someone to actually end up in their own personal fantasy? I'm thinking that's a rare situation. Right? Not in a million years! But, here I am, waking up between two of the most sexy, beautiful men I have ever known in my entire life; all thirty-five years of it, very soon to be thirty-six.

Even in my wildest dreams, and like I said, I have had some wild dreams, I couldn't come up with this scenario. My god, what a difference a year makes. What an absolutely, positively, lovely difference a year makes!

To think, this time last year I was preparing to be alone and making all sorts of decisions that would change my life. I never realized they would bring me to where I am today. Now, I wouldn't have it any other way.

~~~~~~~~~~~~

I was turning thirty-five. To say the least, would be to admit that I wasn't totally happy with where I was in my life and or how I saw things progressing in the near future. I wasn't the type of woman who ever pictured herself with the two point four children, a three bedroom, two bath home and a white picket fence.

Let me say, that there is nothing wrong with that picture. It just wasn't my picture. In my entire life, I don't ever remember having one of those little girl dreams where the wedding dress, flowers, cake, and all that stuff, including Prince Charming were in my future. It never happened that way for me. That wasn't my dream.

Even as a young girl, I pictured myself as the school principal, the business owner, or the best selling author. I always wanted to be the leader. I was never the one who followed someone else's directions or rules, at least not without a debate as to why. Even then, I didn't follow them well. Believe me when I say, it has gotten me in trouble more than a few times. It still does on occasion. Only now I enjoy being in trouble! At least most of the time.

Like I was saying, I was the one who was always in charge. The one the other kids listened to. It didn't change too much as I grew up. I still liked things my way. I gave my own directions. I made my own rules. That explains why I chose to become a freelance writer when the opportunity arose. The key word being "free," not having to follow rules. Well, that's not totally true, there are a few rules. Just much less than in the nine-to-five types of careers.

~~~~~~~~~~~~

There I was, thirty-five and no longer sure I was on the right path. So what should a girl to do? The only thing I could do. The one thing I've always done when things didn't feel right or I wasn't happy. I'd make changes! Rethink what I want, define my goal, make my action plan, and go forth and conquer! The only problem was I wasn't sure what I wanted to conquer.

In order to figure it all out, I decided to have a night out with some of my closest friends. Luckily for me, four of them, four of the people who know me best, had invited me out for dinner to celebrate my birthday. I would get to celebrate and tap their brains about my dilemma. It was a win-win situation.

We met at one of our favorite bar-restaurants. Rembrandt's was an old converted dime store that was one of our places to relax and enjoy ourselves. It was comfortable, the wait staff and bartenders knew us, and most of the regulars were really great people who enjoyed a good time.

We had our usual table in the corner between two walls of windows that faced center city. We were close to the Art Museum, so you could see the cityscape all lit up and it looked spectacular against the night sky. We ordered drinks and started talking. Everyone was wishing me happy birthday and Jen, our favorite waitress, came out with a birthday cake. Someone, who really must not have liked me, actually placed thirty-five candles on it and lit each one.

My friends and the entire population of the bar started to sing Happy Birthday. It can be an emotional moment when so many people are happy for you. The serenade ended and I blew out my candles. Things slowly quieted down and we sat down for dinner.

"I thought we would get through the formalities before we eat." Diane said, as she laughed at me for counting the candles. "So, I asked Jen to bring out the cake first so we could sing Happy Birthday."

Diane was my best friend and sat to my right like a wing-man guarding my six. She was the person who knew me best. We had known each other since our first year at college. We'd both attended the University of Pennsylvania. She was a nursing major and I was English Lit. We met at a freshmen meet and greet and have been best friends ever since. She knows me better than anyone.

During our sophomore year we became roommates and in our junior year we moved off-campus to an apartment in the city. That's how we'd found Rembrandts'. Our first apartment was right across from the Art Museum and Rembrandts' was in walking distance. We ate more dinners and drank more wine there, than we did in our own apartment.

The place was our sanctuary. It was where we let our hair down and had the freedom to say whatever was on our minds. It was our home away from home, our safe place. Anything said at Rembrandts' stayed there.

I really only shared my most personal thoughts with two people, Diane and Brian. My two closest tribe members, my support system. They both knew all there was to know about me. Surprisingly, they both loved me despite that fact.

Brian knew I'd been feeling a little off, but knew it was more than that. Diane knew I'd been feeling a bit lost. She was up-to-date on everything I had been debating over those weeks before everything in my life changed. During dinner, she reached over and squeezed my hand. When I gave her a "what's up" look, she gave me a reassuring smile and a wink. With that she addressed our friends.

"Ok. Everyone, I need your undivided attention. Although we are here to celebrate Olivia's birthday, we have another agenda item." I was staring at her, not sure where she was going with this but trusting her enough to let her go with it. She continued, "My girl," a term of endearment she uses frequently with me, "has a dilemma and needs our help. So, no shitting around, I want you all to listen to her and bring forth your best ideas and suggestions. No jokes! This is serious and she wants our input."

Silence swept over our group. She broke the tension by ending with, "...and you know my girl never asks for anyone else's opinion. So this is some serious shit." Everyone at the table broke into laughter knowing just how true her words were.

"Go ahead Liv. I think we have their attention." Giving my hand another little squeeze, she pulled me up from my chair. That's Di, the one you can count on when you expect it and more importantly, when you don't expect it. And that's one of the reasons Di is my best friend. I can count on her at all times. We have no secrets. She has my back and I have hers. I'm closer to Di than I am my own sister.

Everyone was looking at me as I resumed the conversation. "Well guys, don't look so worried. No one is dying." There was a little nervous laughter, but they still appeared a little worried. I smiled and looked at them.

"You know that you are very special to me. You each have a very important role in my life. I love and respect you very much."

Teary eyed, I continued to speak to a completely silent group. This was a rare event, even for our little gathering. Silence was foreign to us. Rarer was the fact that I had tears in my eyes and they were slowly streaming down my cheeks. I never cried in front of people.

"I want, no, I need to tell you that I love you. I want you to know how much you mean to me."

I looked at some of the people I loved the most in this world. They were all focused on me. Brian was directly to my left. I could tell he was concerned about me because he started adjusting his watch band on his wrist. One of the nervous habits he had whenever we talked about a problem or something that was important to him. I'm one of those things. I'm important to him. Our friendship was more than a simple friendship, it was very special.

When I looked down and caught him playing with his watch, he unexpectedly stood up, hugged me, and kissed my cheek. Leaning in, he whispered, "Whatever you need, I'm here for you. I hope you know that." I kissed him back, smiled and he sat back down.

Brian and I had dated for several months the previous year and had kept a friends with benefits relationship since then. We loved each other, we were just not in love with each other at the time. But we were pretty good together when it came to the bedroom, and a few other rooms we trialed. Yes, believe it or not, it was that unique relationship where a man and a woman could remain friends after dating and having sex with each other. Ok, so, we still had sex with each other. I never said it was perfect, or platonic, did I?

I gathered my thoughts again and continued talking after Brian's kiss. Every now and then, I felt his hand run up the back of my thigh and pat my bottom. It was his supportive touch. His way of reassuring me. It worked. I refocused my thoughts and continued.

"I've talked with each of you at one time or another about life circumstances and how the choices we make affect our lives. We've all had those deep discussions questioning who we are, who we're supposed to be, and are we doing what we're meant to be doing. The ones that usually start over a glass of wine and end sometime around two or three o'clock in the morning." I took a few seconds and looked at my closest friends, my support system, my family, before I continued.

"Recently, I realized that I am not happy with the way things are for me. It's as simple as that. So, I've decided to make some major changes. Originally, I thought I would ask you for your opinions and some ideas. That's what Diane was referring to." I peeked down first at Di and then over to Brian and I felt stronger.

"After feeling the love and support from each of you, I have all I need to finalize my decision. I've decided to give up my apartment and do some traveling. I can write from anywhere and I don't have any commitments that are keeping me here right now, so it's a good time for me.

"I was reading an article a few days ago and I read a quote from a young author. Some of you may be familiar with her writings. Her name is Marie Lu and she wrote the Legend series. What she said, made something inside me come alive and, to be cliche, it was like a lightening strike. Immediately, I knew I wanted to do something totally different from what I'm doing now.

"She said, 'Each day means a new twenty-four hours. Each day means everything's possible again. You live in the moment, you die in the moment, and you take it all one day at a time.' " As I looked around the table, everyone was nodding in agreement.

"I've always wanted to go across country and just stop wherever I wanted and spend some time exploring. I think this is the perfect time to do it. I've decided to 'live in the moment,' as they say. If I wait any longer, I'll start to think that I'm too old or find some other reason not to." I smiled before I continued, "While I'm traveling, I'm going to start that novel I always wanted to write."

I fondly gazed at the people who had come to mean so much to me and for a split second, I thought to myself, Can I do this? Can I leave them and basically start over? I realized I could. I thought to myself, Yes, I can and if I fail, they will take me back with open arms.

"So, that's my big birthday announcement. I'm leaving Philly in a few weeks and going exploring. If I'm lucky, I may find out some things about myself. Who knows, it may completely change my life! Of course, I might also be back here in a few months asking for a couch to sleep on."

They all laughed. I heard everything from "You know you will succeed at anything you do," to "Whatever you do or whatever you need we are all here for you."

The great thing was I know that they meant it. These people had been part of my family for years and I knew that would not change. No matter where I went, they would always be home.

~~~~~~~~

After I kissed everyone good-bye and said good-night, I grabbed my bag and headed for the door with a box of birthday cake in hand. As I was leaving, I saw Brian leaning up against my car, waiting. Since we had been touching each other all night long, I wasn't surprised to see him there. We had started with the hug and kiss, then the hand holding through dinner, then him caressing my thigh through dessert, ending with my hand rubbing his cock during the after dinner drinks. Like I said, friends with benefits.

"Hey little girl, do you want some candy?" My eyes teared again at the thought of missing him. At the same time, I heard myself laugh because that's what I said to him the first time we met.

We were at a tavern on South Street and I saw him standing, leaning back against the bar. His pose was similar to this one, him leaning against my car. He was standing, all tall, dark and sexy. I could have just eaten him up. At the time, I thought, I just might do that a little later.

Anyway, I walked up to him at the bar that first night and got his attention. Then I peered into his eyes, smiled, and said in a deeply sexy voice, "Hey little boy, do you want some candy?" and I waited. He actually made me wait before he answered.

"Little girl, you don't know what you're asking. If I were to say yes, what kind of candy do you have for me?" He actually growled. "I'm well known for my sweet tooth."

Damn, he was sexy that night, and that was the start of our relationship.

I found him even sexier now. Maybe it was because he was more relaxed around me. It could have been because he knew me and I knew him. More likely it was because we had a bond that was different from any other friendship or bond either one of us had ever shared. Regardless of the reason, I adored him and I

was fairly sure, he adored me.

"No mister, I can't take any of your candy. I'm not supposed to talk to strange men," I said sweetly, playing it coy. Licking my lips, I teased him a little. Tilting my head to the side, I tossed my hair over my shoulder and in a quiet, innocent sounding voice, I asked, "Umm...What kind of candy do you have? I do like candy."

He pulled me close to his chest and smirked. Wrapping his arms around me, he kissed my mouth fully and hard. There was no warm up. We had taken care of that during dinner. His lips were warm, soft, and oh so delicious. I could still taste the birthday cake on them when I sucked the bottom one into my mouth. When his tongue entered my mouth and started to explore, I tasted the shot of Patron that we all did to finish the night. I didn't know if I was feeling the heat from his tongue or the heat from the tequila, but whatever it was, it was good.

No, make that great. The warmth went from my tongue and down my throat as if I was doing another shot. It then rested in the lower part of me.

It was a deep kiss, penetrating not only my mouth, but my heart and soul. I gave the intensity and the heat right back. He knew I wanted him, he knew I loved him. I knew he felt the same way about me. In a more perfect world, we might have had the happily ever after, but it wasn't to be, at least not in the foreseeable future.

Ours was an easy relationship. The kind you can come back to after a while and pick up like it was yesterday. We enjoyed each other intellectually, emotionally, and physically. We were of similar minds, but the happily ever after stuff was never part of our picture. We both agreed to that from the start.

Brian made a deep sigh after our kiss. I refocused on what he was saying. "Oh, honey, I know you like candy," he more or less growled out. "I'm going to give you all the candy you can handle." He kissed the tip of my nose. "All you have to do is tell me what you want and I'll do my best to give it to you."

"Promise?" I said, as I licked my tongue over his bottom lip.

"I promise. But you have to promise to tell me exactly what you want. Otherwise, no candy, no anything." He winked. "Understand?"

"Yes," I sighed.

"It's your birthday and I plan on giving you everything you've ever told me you wanted," he teased.

"Everything?" I was curious at that little crooked smile of his. It only showed up when he had done something I wasn't going to be happy with or if he had something up his sleeve and was trying to convince me it was a good idea. This time, I wasn't sure which it was.

"Yes, everything," he said, "but you have to ask for it." His attitude was a little self assured.

"Ok. I promise I'll ask."

My head was spinning a little from a combination of emotions, alcohol, and lust. But more from the lust side of the equation. It wasn't a bad combination from where I was standing. The problem was, it wasn't the best combination to have when I was trying to figure out what he was up to.

"Good. Now, give me your keys, you've had more to drink than I have," he said, and he put his hand out for them.

I hadn't had that much to drink. He was being all masculine and guy-like. I remembered how much I liked it when he was like that. I handed him the keys and he opened the passenger door for me.

"You break it; you bought it," I said as I got in.

"Get that beautiful ass in the car so I can get you home and wish you a real happy birthday."

He gave my ass a playful smack, just hard enough to make me squeal. I waited until he was in before I asked about what he was up to. He was acting way too suspicious.

"Did you get me a present?" I asked in an innocent manner.

"Honey, I have more than one present for you. Don't worry about that." He was looking at me with those big brown puppy dog eyes and then all of a sudden, they looked more like the eyes of a wolf. They were all shiny and focused. Licking his lips like he was starving, he looked like he was hunting prey.

That predatory look of his was making me hot. If I wasn't getting damp panties in the bar as he stroked along my thigh, I was making up for that now. A few great kisses and some sexy innuendos and I was slipping over my leather car seat in my rather wet panties.

"Get me home James, I think I need to change my undies."

"There will be no panties tonight," he laughed. "Once those are off, you won't be in need of any for the rest of the night."

Reaching over me, he grabbed the seat belt and buckled me into the belt lock. His forearm grazed my breast as he pulled the belt and he kissed me. A kiss that was full of promise as his hand dipped into my blouse and stroked my breast.

Immediately my nipple became erect. Brian slid his thumb over it, stroking my little nub hard while the rest of my breast rested in his hand. He caressed it back and forth and I could feel the callus on the outer edge of his thumb rough against my nipple.

His skin was hard and rough in that one spot and he was rubbing it across my engorged bud over and over. The friction of it was causing my nipple to get warm and tender. The pain was a mixed feeling. One that kind of hurt, but at the same time, felt good. I loved it and his touch was sending little shockwaves through my body. I didn't want him to stop.

When he pulled back from the kiss and lightly bit my lower lip, I purred. The nip he took was firm enough to cause a little whimper to escape between breaths. His touch caused those shocks to be sent through my body, straight to my pussy. He was killing me. My head was back, against the headrest and I couldn't stop repeating the word yes. He looked at me as he took his thumb away and gave my breast a squeeze. Withdrawing his hand from my blouse, he smiled as I quietly cried out to him, "No, don't stop now."

"Liv, if I don't stop now, I'm not going to be able to stop at all. By the look in your eyes and on that beautiful face, I might just give you one of your birthday gifts right here on the front seat." He laughed teasingly.

"Would that be so bad? Besides, it's my birthday and it's my front seat."

"Yeah, Liv, but it's my birthday gift. I'm not giving it to you until we get home. So live with it, baby," he said all stern and domineering.

"Do I have any other choice?" I asked, but it came out sounding more like a pout than anything else.

"Yes, but I don't think you would be willing to do 'that' in your car." He looked at me and laughed again, while he started the engine.

"Don't be too sure about that. Besides, are you sure that I haven't done 'that' in my car already." I stuck my tongue out at him and he tried to grab it.

"No baby, I'm not completely sure about that. But I am sure that you will pay for that little tongue maneuver you just pulled," he said as he cocked his brow at me.

A few minutes later we drove up my street. We got to my apartment building and pulled into the parking garage. Brian came around the car and opened my door. Reaching in, he took my hand to help me out. I wasn't drunk and I could have opened my own door, but he helped me out of the car like he always did. He also opened doors to buildings and let me enter first. I loved that. It was one of those little things he did that set him apart from other men I had dated. Most guys don't open a girl's door anymore.

Getting out, I was guided by his hand on the small of my back. You would think an independent woman like me wouldn't like the car door being opened, or the guy wanting to drive me home, or the hand helping me out, but I did. I may be independent, but there are certain things that just made me feel more of a woman. Unique things he did that made me think of him like more of a man, a chivalrous and sexy man.

We arrived at the garage elevator and he pushed the call button. Seconds later the doors opened. Brian escorted me in and pushed the button for the eighth-floor. His hand was still on my lower back, but inched its way down. He used his arm at my back to half turn me so that we were looking at each other. Positioned in the back corner, his body was blocking me, and the security camera couldn't see what he was doing behind me. He started to rub my ass cheek in a circular motion. On every third circle, he grasped it a little harder than the time before. When he grasped my ass, he'd pull me forward and rub his groin up against me. I could feel his cock hardening in his pants as he whispered against the side of my head.

"Liv, when I get you into the apartment, do you know what I'm going to do?"

"No," I whispered back. "But I'd like to," I said all breathy sounding. He'd had me hot and bothered since we were at Rembrandts'.

I could barely get the stupid words out of my mouth because I was afraid I was going to come right there in the damn elevator. His hand slid so far down my ass, it was between my legs and he was pushing his fingers upward. All I felt was the heat of his hand, the pressure of his fingers, and his warm breath in my ear. God, I wanted him inside me, I needed him to take me, and I was dying for him to make me come.

Desperate for more, I started rocking back on his hand to increase the pressure, the pleasure. My breathing was getting faster. I felt every pulse site in my body and not one was throbbing as badly as my pussy. Each heartbeat was so strong, I felt it pulse throughout my body. The sound it made in my head was deafening. The throbbing beat throughout my body was so loud, I couldn't think straight. The pulsing beat was no longer coming from my heart, but from my sex.

I had such a needy feeling in my pussy that I had to hold my legs tightly together or I thought I would orgasm right in the elevator. I could no longer control the beat between my legs, clenching my muscles tighter, only may it worse. My body was betraying me. My panties were soaked and I could smell my own scent of arousal. Brian just kept whispering dirty, sexy things into my ear. I hadn't heard much of what he'd said after the first few sentences. I realized he stopped with the finger maneuvers and was looking at me like he was waiting for me to do something.

"What? What are you waiting for?" I asked.

Now, he was laughing at me. I was dying to get my hands on him and my man was actually laughing at me. If I wasn't in such a sexually needy state, I would have kicked his ass for laughing at me.

"Liv, you haven't heard a word I've said, have you?" he asked as he swatted my bottom firmly.

"Yes. I heard you say, 'Do you know what I'm going to do to you?' or something like that." I was frustrated and strung a little tight, and it came out louder and a little harsher than I planned.

"Liv, I said a lot more after that!" He was holding the door open button.

"Well, it's your fault I couldn't hear you with your hand practically inside me and that constant tapping of your finger.

You're driving me crazy!" I looked at him a little annoyed, a little in question of what he was up to and of what he was waiting for from me. "Now, what are you waiting for?" I kind of yelled at him because he had made me so sexually frustrated with his finger probe.

"Well, baby, I'm waiting for you to get out. I've been holding the doors open for a while now. If we get out, I can let these people go up to their floor." He nodded his head toward the other side of the elevator. In the back corner I saw a young couple that I recognized from a few floors up. I never even realized they'd got on the elevator with us.

Brian's smile was so smug, I wanted to punch him. Instead, I apologized to the couple and walked out of the elevator as steadily as possible given my aroused state. As the doors closed, I heard the young woman laughing as her boyfriend said, "Baby, do you know what I'm going to do to you..." the doors closed.

Brian was still laughing. "Come on Liv, let me get you in that apartment and really celebrate your birthday." Opening the door, he walked me in.

The door closed. He flipped the security lock. Immediately he had me up against the wall, his mouth on mine. The warmth from his body was seeping into me as he was grinding against me. My arms wrapped around his neck and he lifted me off the floor. Grabbing my right leg, he pulled it up to his thigh, and ground his pelvis into me. I felt his cock rub hard over my pubic mound. Grinding and grinding, the pressure never gave up. It just kept building higher and higher, like climbing up a cliff one step at a time, knowing that once you got to the top you would freefall back down.

I couldn't take it anymore, reaching down, I ran my hand over his swollen cock. I gave him a squeeze. He moaned, a soulful moan from deep in his gut. He reached down and slowly pulled my hand away. Holding my wrist, he pushed my arm against the wall and held it over my head.

"Do you really think you deserve to be rewarded after speaking to me like that in the elevator? You know I don't like to be spoken to like that, especially not in front of others, Olivia." He shook his head, "That was not good behavior." He licked my face. "Neither was sticking your tongue out at me." He licked me again. "What happens when you behave badly Olivia?"

"I get a birthday present?" I giggled. I loved the light spiritedness a little tequila gave me.

"No, try again." He was all deep and sexy sounding, but I heard a little laugh in his voice.

"A punishment?" I questioned giddily.

"Yes, a punishment. I won't forget that. Will you?" he asked, and waited for my response.

"No." I answered quietly. I loved when Brian was in this kind of mood. "Do I still get my birthday gifts?" I gave him my best smile.

"Good, I'm glad you won't forget. Yes, you still get your birthday gifts." He shook his head as if he couldn't believe I just asked that. With that, he pushed my body up the wall with the force of his, he held me there.

He had me lifted so far off the floor I could look him directly in the eyes. Sweat had formed across his brow, his eyes gleamed, and his breath was coming in bunches. He wanted sex as much as I did.

"Brian, are you still going to give me what you promised? Are you going to give me everything I've ever asked for from you?" I could only imagine what that entailed, but it excited me for some reason.

"Well because it is your birthday, I will keep my promise. But, I will also punish you." He smiled and kissed the tip of my nose. It was something I usually hated, but since it might have been one of the last times he did it, I felt kind of nostalgic about the loving act.

"Thank you Brian." I leaned my head forward and caught his chin with a kiss. I looked at him as contrite as I could before I asked, "Can we please start? What are we waiting for? When are you going to tell me what you got me for my birthday?"

"Olivia, you are so impatient." He laughed and then looked at me rather seriously. "I'm just waiting for you to keep your promise."

I was impatient, we had been all over each other for the last hour. He was driving me crazy and he thought I was impatient. "What promise? What are you talking about?"

"Olivia, you promised to tell me what you wanted. I promised to give it to you. Honey, all I'm waiting for is you. What is it you want?"

"Oh God, Brian you're killing me. Do you really need me to tell you what to do?"

"No Olivia. I didn't say tell me what to do. I said, tell me what you want. Those are two different things." He was going all controlling now. Semantics play a big role in his controlling mode and in his teacher mode.

I was losing my patience. Without thinking about the consequences, I reached up with my free hand and pulled his hair back. He grunted and air exited his lungs forcefully. Now his face wasn't so close and I could look him directly in his eyes. Slowly and with all the authority I could muster, I heard myself say, "I want you... I want you to kiss me... I want you to lick me...Brian, I want you to eat me, fuck me, and roll me over and do it again!" I bit at his chin and continued, "Then I want my birthday presents."

He laughed hard. A deep belly laugh came out, yet it sounded sexy coming from him. "Ok honey, just remember you said that. Also remember you pulled my hair because even though I enjoy your initiative, you WILL pay for that."

I could see in his eyes and facial expression, he meant it.

Bam! He threw me over his shoulder, slapped my ass, and headed to the bedroom. Chivalry be damned, he tossed me in the middle of the bed and only my knees and lower legs hung off the side. He pulled off my heels and tossed them to the side. He reached up to my waist and undid my button and zipper. I lifted my hips to help as he pulled my jeans down to my thighs. Once they were down, Brian grabbed me behind both knees and lifted up until my ankles were in his hands. He grasped the legs of my jeans and pulled them off completely. He let my legs gently fall back to the floor and grabbed both of my hands. Roughly, he pulled me up until I was standing right up against his chest.

"Make a list of what else you want Olivia, while I get the rest of these clothes off." Sliding his fingers over the front of my blouse, he practically tore the buttons from their holes. With every unfastened button, he drew his fingers further down the center of my chest and abdomen. His touch was so light, but I didn't know if it was leaving a trail of fire or ice as it caressed my skin. The sensations were mixing, all I knew was I wanted more.

Now my blouse was unbuttoned, his hands caressed back up the path they'd just traced and his fingers dragged across my collarbone until he was able to push the silk blouse over my shoulders. The cool fabric slid down my arm as Brian's tongue slid across first one breast than the other. The feelings of the silk and his tongue were similar, but his tongue was leaving a warm wet streak across my chest. He pushed me back a little and his intense stare examined me from head to toe.

I could tell by the look of hunger in his eyes, he liked what he saw. Stroking my hair, he reached back to release the clip holding it in a ponytail. He tossed the clip on the dresser and ran his fingers through my dense dark brown hair. He took a thick tress and brought it to his nose, breathing in the scent.

"Magnolia's?" he asked, and I nodded yes.

He pushed me back until my knees were against the bed. Letting go of my hair, he traced both hands down the sides of my face. His touch was soft and gentle, but his facial expression was intense. Stopping to give my lips the lightest of kisses, he hesitated before he spoke.

"You may be a brat at times, but your sweetness makes it worth the trouble."

His hands continued over my shoulders, his fingers tracing soft little circles as he moved down my body. When his thumbs touched the outer sides of my breasts, he left my arms and started to trace the rim of my bra. Drawing his fingertips along the lacy pattern, he rested his hands against my chest between my breasts. I felt the light touch of his fingers as they left lines of heat as he traced back and forth.

A look of deep concentration covered his face as he unhooked the front clasp and pulled the cups of my bra back, exposing the fullness of my breasts. Removing it totally, he bent to kiss each mound, leaving quick little kisses over the tops of each breast. The kisses were so light and so gentle, it was like a butterfly's wings flittering along my soft peaks.

He placed one hand behind my neck. Pushing me back, he guided my body down to the bed as his own followed. His body was heavy, but I was used to his weight on top of me. I enjoyed the feeling of him on me. I sighed as the butterfly was gone from my breast and was replaced by the bumble bee as he began to tease.

Brian had one nipple in his mouth and was sucking on it in hard short bursts. The other nipple had come to attention under his callused thumb. They were so tender, I knew I wouldn't be able to take his teasing for too long. His suckling was like little bee stings when he pulled his mouth from my nipple and it literally made a "pop" sound as he released it.

"Brian please, Brian, I can't take much more of this teasing." He continued until I cried out a little and bucked my pelvis up against him. "Brian please," I was practically begging with him.

He pinched one nipple, while his mouth nipped on the other and I cried out again, "Oh, fuck me!"

"Oh, baby, I will!" he said in a deep sexy voice.

Standing up, he started to remove his clothes, never taking his eyes from mine. My nipples were so hot and tender, they hurt. I went to put my hands over them to cool them off and provide a little comfort, but he yelled at me. Well, not yelled so much as directed me not to.

"No Olivia. Do not touch them, they're mine tonight. You're mine tonight. Do you understand?"

A chill ran through my body at the sound of his voice, his words. My mind was focused on him and I knew when he called me Olivia that things had just changed course. He had gone from being "easy going Brian" to "let's play Brian." Both Brians' were great, but "let's play Brian" didn't like to leave room for interpretation.

"Yes Brian," I moaned more than answered.

He pulled off his shirt and his bare chest was beautiful, no hair, just clean soft skin and a little muscle. He was lean, but he had the body of an athlete. My eyes raked over his well-formed chest, over his abs, and then down to my favorite part. That muscle that only some men have developed. The muscle that extends from the upper portions of a man's hip and goes down and inward to his pelvis. I always thought of them as arrows pointing to his cock.

I loved to trace that muscle with my tongue. It fascinated me and was the biggest turn on for him. He kept his eyes on me, watching me as I focused on him. I had always loved to see him undress. It was like watching a Christmas present being unwrapped. In this case, it was a birthday present. It looked pretty in the wrapping, but it was more fun to play with when unwrapped and out of the box.

Brian slid his thumbs inside the waist of his pants. He took his time gliding them forward to the button of his jeans. I licked my lips and he hesitated. Damn, he was going to tease me, make me wait. He pulled his hands from his jeans and bent to take off his shoes and socks. He took his time before he stood up, damn but this man was sexy. Every move he made while undressing was sexy and turning me on even more.

Brian was tall, he stood about six-four. He was a teacher, but he played basketball and kept in decent shape since college. He was pure lean muscle. His body was like a Ryan Lochte swimmer's body. He even looked a little like Ryan with his wavy dark hair, brown eyes and big smile. Brian was a swimmer and a basketball player in high school, receiving a partial scholarship to play for Temple's basketball team. He still had the body of a college athlete and I enjoyed looking at him, clothed or unclothed.

I pulled him toward me and gave him a long deep kiss. I thought of all the things I would miss, and realized it would be Brian's kisses that I would miss the most. It was as if when our lips meet, all was right in the world. Depending on how we kissed, so many things were communicated. Right at that moment, it was thank you and I'm going to miss you so much. On top of that, it was I want you.

When we broke, he looked into my eyes for a few seconds before his hands stroked my face and moved down my neck, over my arms and continued down my body. He leaned down and placing them on the outside of my knees. He still hadn't stopped looking into my eyes. It was unnerving how long he could hold his stare. It was also damn attractive and sexy.

His hands were big and his fingers were long. They were the strongest looking hands I had ever seen. I loved the way they looked and how they felt on my body. They were not always gentle but they definitely knew what they were doing. He started to stroke up my outer thighs and then down again, alternating pressure as his hands covered the surface of my legs. God, I loved his touch.

He repositioned himself in front of me. This time, when he got back down to my knees, he slid his hands to the insides of my legs. Again he slid up my thighs lightly dragging his nails up the inside and then drew the pads of his fingers back down. Every time he reached my knees, he'd spread my thighs a little more. When my knees were spread apart, he dropped down between my legs. He was so tall that his waist and chest cleared the top edge of the bed and all I could think of was kissing every inch of him. I squeezed him between my legs, holding him there. I could feel the rough touch of his jeans between my lower legs.

He slid his hands back up my thighs and stopped when his thumbs were barely an inch away from my pussy. His thumbs were making the small circles I was so used to. His touch altered between soft and firm. The softness and tickle excited me, but his firmer grip allowed me to release myself to him and his hold. His fingers were applying more pressure to my outer legs as he became more aroused by what he was doing to me. As I felt his grip sink deeper into my fleshy thighs, I knew I would have little bruised finger marks there the next day.

Brian took a deep breath in and the look in his eyes changed. I knew he scented my arousal. I could smell it myself and it was erotic knowing how much it turned him on. Without any warning, he dropped his head to my lower abdomen and stayed there. His forehead was lying on my pubic mound like it was a pillow and his nose was buried in the crotch of my panties.

Oh God, he was such a tease. This was part of my punishment. I knew what his plan was for me. He would torture me and make me wait until he felt like I had suffered enough. He was lying there breathing in my scent. I wasn't sure what to do. He wasn't saying anything. He was slowly breathing in and releasing his hot breath over my sex. My body started to tremble. My nerve endings were firing from head to toe.

I needed something to hold on to. I reached for Brian's head. In my mind, I heard the words, No, don't. They were too late to stop me. My hands were moving of their own volition.

"No Olivia, don't do it. Don't move," he whispered.

I was in mid-motion, but I stopped. I remembered thinking, Should I move them back or stay still? I'm not sure which option is better. He had me so highly aroused, I was surprised I knew my own name. He just lay there, breathing in and out, while I was slowly dying for release.

"Olivia, place your arms above your head," he said, as he peeked up at me and licked his lips.

I did as he asked and placed my hands above my head. Finally, he started to move. But this was worse. He was slowly rubbing his nose over my panties, tracing the slit of my pussy. Oh God, I wanted him to move, but not like that. He lifted his head a little and replaced his nose with his tongue. His warm, wet tongue was now pressing my already wet panties between my swollen lips. I tried not to make a sound, but it was useless.

"Oh God, Brian please, please." My body stretched to meet his tongue and I felt my muscles tighten in my ass and thighs. The anticipation of his next move, in combination with my creative mind, was making me crazy with need.

He lifted his head and looked at me again. I begged him to stop teasing me, between my panted breaths, "Please Brian, stop teasing."

"Olivia, I haven't even started to tease you and we haven't even started to go through your original list." He nipped my labia between his teeth. "Remember, kiss me, touch me, lick me, etc... etc.. I'm working my way through it, now be a good girl and be patient for me. You will be patient for me, won't you Olivia?" he asked, his eyes dark gleaming and his sexy smile teasing me as he spoke.

"I'm trying, baby. I'm trying, but it's been a long night of your teasing and my being patient," I said, as he laughed at me.

"It's going to be a little longer baby. I plan on keeping you occupied until I'm ready to give you the rest of your birthday presents," he said. There was a sly look on his face. He was definitely up to something, I could feel it. "What do you think about that?" he asked.

I nodded, knowing I didn't have any real choice in the matter. I looked at him and nodded again, I wanted to make sure I didn't miss anything he said while my imagination was at work.

"Good girl." He pushed my knees together, "Hips up." I raised my hips and he pulled my panties off. I could feel how wet they were as he drew them down my legs. They were practically sticking to me. When he got them off, he held them to his nose and took a deep breath in. "I love the way you smell."

I lay there completely naked with my legs spread eagled and my juices slowly running down the path of my ass to the bed linen beneath me. Brian was standing there watching me. His eyes were focused on my pussy as the slick fluid slowly seeped from between my labia. He undid his jeans, pulling them off and tossing them on the growing pile of clothes. He wasn't wearing underwear and his cock jutted out as soon as his jeans passed over it.

Brian's cock was beautiful. It was thick and perfectly shaped. I could see the shiny purple head as he took his hand and encircled it and looked at me. He kept his cock free of hair and the rest of his pubic area was clipped very short. Slowly he slid his hand up and down and a small amount of pearly fluid came out. He took his fingers, wiped the fluid from the tip, and then brought them to my lips.

"Happy Birthday Olivia," he said. He licked his own lips as he glided his fingers along with mine.

I opened my mouth and licked his fingers clean. He had a very salty taste. It was like a taste of the ocean. It was strong, but not bad. He tasted good, like a man should taste, strong and lingering.

Dropping back down to his knees, he placed his torso between my spread legs. He bent until I could only see from his eyes up as he kissed my pubic mound. Kissing the inside of my upper thighs, he swirled his tongue in a curvy wavelike motion. Back and forth, he gave each thigh his attention until his cheek rubbed against my sex. He stopped and held my gaze.

Placing his tongue on my perineum, he slowly licked upwards. His tongue felt warm, silky, and wet as he collected the juices that had accumulated. Watching him do that to me was like watching him lick an ice cream cone that was melting. Taking his time. Licking up and down my fold slowly, carefully, not missing an inch. I could feel his soft tongue lapping at my juices. It was slow, deliberately so, and the tip of his tongue touched me ever so lightly, gently. It felt like a feather being drawn over my skin, at first it felt good, very good. After a while though, I needed it to stop. It was too much sensation.

I needed him to stop, but I knew he wouldn't. He was waiting for me to move so he could start all over again. I held still long enough that he stopped after a few more minutes.

"Very good Olivia," his brow raised up, "I thought I had you for a moment. I know you were close to flinching. Very well done," he said, as he thought of what else he could do to tease me and push me closer to the edge. "Let's see how well you continue to do. Let's see if you can hold out until your presents arrive?"

Oh, God. One second I was so happy he'd stopped and the next, I knew I was in more trouble.

Watching my face intently, he slid his thumbs to the base of my labia. I couldn't hold on for much longer and I knew it, so did he. At first he drew his thumbs up and down my fold, then he opened my lips and inserted just the tips of his thumbs as he continued the pattern. He pushed in a little more and his fatty callused thumb pads were caressing the insides of my sex, moving up and down the inner walls of my lips. It was mind blowing, the feeling of his rough skin against my soft folds was causing a pleasure I couldn't describe. I didn't have much longer. I was so wet, so wanton. As much as, I hated those long drawn out teases, I loved them more, and Brian knew it.

Sliding the length of his thumbs along my labial folds, he held me open. I could feel the cool air against the inner warmth of my sex. He bent his head, licking me with just the tip of his tongue as he kept it curled in a U shape. It went up and down touching every silken inner surface of my pussy. Every crease and crevice was licked, he made sure of that. Cupping my clit in the U fold of his tongue, he quickly teased my sensitive little clit left and right.

My body tensed, my mind focused on every sensation he caused me. As my thighs flexed tight, my pelvis lifted to meet Brian's mouth. My neck and back arched as goosebumps covered my body. I felt little firebolts cross my clit as my hands went to my nipples. I needed more, so I started to rub and pinch my nipples hard. As Brian worked his magic between my legs, I kept my nipples erect and sensitive.

I couldn't take it anymore and I cried out again. "Brian, please make me come, please let me come."

Immediately, he placed his mouth over my clit and encircled it tightly between his pursed lips. Sliding his fingers into my sex, he matched the motion of his mouth while I continued to pinch my nipples. Sucking hard and fast, he started a different attack. My head cleared a little and I realized the sucking sound he was making was in a rhythmic tone. It was repetitive. I recognized that tune. Oh god, I thought, he's sucking me off to the Happy Birthday song.

All control was lost as my body shook, my legs tightened around Brian's head, my hips bucked up, and I tried to shake him loose. Instead, I ended up pulling him closer. Without missing a beat, he kept sucking my clit to Happy Birthday. It was fucking torture and I let him know it.

"Fuck Brian...fuck...me...fuck."

I couldn't hold back. His tongue and mouth teased and tortured my clit, fingers slid in and out of my vagina rapidly. I felt his teeth nip at my sex bud. I yelled, "Brian, I'm going to come. I have to, I, I, I can't..."

He held my sensitized clit between his tongue and the back of his teeth. The intense pressure and his pulsating sucking was torture to me. I achieved my long awaited orgasm and came all over his chin. It felt like it was never going to stop as my body continued to tremble and my hips thrashed side-to-side. Reaching up, he placed his forearm across my pelvis to hold me down. His mouth never left my clit and he never stopped sucking. He finished the last verse of "Happy Birthday to you" while I tried to catch my breath and waited for the shaking in my limbs to stop.

Before I completely came down from my climax, I saw his head pop up from between my legs, his lower face and chin were soaked. We gazed into each other's eyes as I tried to catch my breath. Before I had a chance to gain control of my body, Brian placed the tip of his middle finger on my vagina. Slowly he started to encircle my opening, tracing it over and over.

I could feel my muscles contract, my breathing beginning to catch in my chest once again. I was so sensitive that any little touch to my sex sent off shock waves. I was biting my lower lip to prevent myself from making any moves. It felt so good I didn't want to lose this feeling. He was edging me and I knew if I moved, it would be difficult to reach this level of intensity again. I fought my own instincts and held very still.

The tip of his finger slid just inside me and I tightened my thighs and buttocks holding him tight. He made a swirling action with his finger and pushed it into the first knuckle. Pushing in and out again, he slid his finger against my wet flesh. I held back a cry. A cry of want, need and frustration. I wanted to come a second time.

Brian knew how to torture me, taking his time, he pushed in a little further. Never taking his eyes from mine, he teased me mercilessly, sliding his finger in and out of me. He'd swirl it to the right, then the left as he thrust it in and out, picking up speed. It was like a game of who would blink first and he was very good at games. I was clenched so tight I could feel each knuckle of his finger as he continued to play with me.

I remained silent, but from my neck down, every muscle in my body was contracted and my legs started to twitch. I gave in and closed my eyes. He slid his finger all the way in and started thrusting it quickly, in and out, in and out. He added his index finger and upped his pace. Drawing his finger along my front wall, he tapped on that spongy area just under my pubic bone.

His thumb was placed over my clit, rubbing it up and down with each thrust of his fingers. My clit was so tender, I felt like it was on fire as he played with me. The throbbing in my pussy was out of control, the electrical pulsations of my clit were their own form of self torture. My muscle fibers were strung so tight, it felt like I was going to burst. Every feeling I had was so intense, I thrust forward and upward so that I could feel more pressure and take his fingers into me deeper and harder. Suddenly, he stopped.

"No, Brian I'm sorry, I couldn't help it." I was panting like I'd just run a marathon and my heart was beating out of my chest.

"What did I say about moving?" he growled.

I could barely speak between gasps, "Not to...move...unless...you tell... me to?" I was trying not to cry and trying to relax my muscles. It was difficult to hold it together.

"And yet you moved. Did I tell you, you could move?" His voice was strict, yet gentle in its control. I could hear the underlying desire in it.

"No."

"Olivia, you are one lucky girl." He licked his lips and smirked at me. "Since it's your birthday tonight, you get a free pass," his brow arched as he continued, "but you only get one pass baby. Understand?" He kissed my tummy.

"Yes, Brian."

He was about to say something when my doorbell rang. Not once, but three consecutive times. I looked at the bedside clock and saw it was almost one in the morning. I looked at Brian, as if to question who it could be, but there was a gleam in his eye and that sly smile he had earlier reappeared.

"Happy Birthday, Olivia," he cleared his throat, trying to gain control. He sounded as if he was expecting the interruption which again made me suspicious.

"Brian. What did you do?"

"Exactly what I said I would," he told me, as he tossed his shirt at me and pulled on his jeans. "Put this on and answer the door."

"Brian, what is it?" I sat on the side of the bed trying to calm my body down as I pulled on his shirt, buttoned it, and folded up his sleeves a bit.

"It's the rest of your present. I told you I planned to make your every wish come true. Well, I have a special surprise for you tonight. A combination birthday present, happy travels present, and a don't forget me present all rolled into one."

"You got someone to make a delivery at this time of night?" I was surprised.

"I made special arrangements with a very special deliveryman to make sure I could give you exactly what you wanted." He smiled and slapped my butt before continuing, "It's something we talked about not too long ago."

"Brian, we talked about a lot of things in the past few weeks. When exactly?" I finished buttoning his shirt and looked him in the eyes. "What are you up to?"

"You'll see soon enough. It will all be clear to you as soon as you open the door. Now let's go answer that bell, shall we?" he said and patted my butt again as if we weren't just about ready to jump each other.

I had no idea what it was, but I was sure it was going to be amazing and over the top if he'd made special arrangements to have it delivered. Plus, he must have paid a pretty penny for the special delivery charge.

I walked down the hall with Brian following directly behind me. I could feel the wetness between my legs as my lips slid against each other. I looked back and smiled, "Baby, there's not much I can do to cover up my excitement, but you might want to pull those jeans up a little more and zip them. I doubt the delivery person wants to see you in all your glory." I started to flip the safety lock open and undo the bolt. I was about to peek through the security view when Brian put his hand on my shoulder and shook his head no.

I opened the door and was surprised to see it was Paul, Brian's roommate. As soon as he smiled at me, thoughts of something

I told Brian a few weeks ago, came rushing back into my thoughts. I closed my eyes and took a step back, praying what I was thinking wasn't true. I bumped right into Brian's chest. I heard him laugh quietly in my ear as his hands grasped my arms as if to catch me and hold me up.

When I looked at Paul, his face had that Cheshire cat smile. It was that look that said he knew a little too much information about me. I peeked over my shoulder and Brian had that same sly smile. I was at a loss. I didn't know what to do or to say. I flashed back and remembered lying in bed one morning and talking, after a rather active night of lovemaking with Brian.

We were holding each other and talking about our night and what we liked, what we felt, and how much fun we had together. As usual, one thing led to another and Brian started to play with my breasts and trace my nipples. I remember exactly what he said that morning.

"Liv, baby, tell me your wildest fantasy. Tell me something you've never told another man," he said, as he kissed my ear and continued to stroke my body.

We were just sharing, telling each other our secrets and our fantasies. It wasn't unusual for us to talk about these types of things, especially after a night of fun sex. I didn't think twice about sharing my intimate thoughts with him. So, I started telling Brian about my ultimate sex fantasy. It was one of those random thoughts that became a recurrent dream and a major fantasy theme. Each time I had it, it became more detailed. Oh Lord, the details were amazing and I couldn't figure out why my subconscious mind kept returning to this one fantasy.

Every time I had this dream, I'd wake up and spend the next hour, trying to analyze it. It was annoying and a little frustrating.

My mind would race through a dozen questions. Some with no specific answers. I would lay there thinking, Why this fantasy? Why two men? Why Brian's best friend?

"My wildest fantasy...hmm. Let me think..." I said, as he continued to drag his fingers down my chest, over my abdomen, and rested his hand between my legs.

"Don't think Liv, just tell me," he whispered into my neck as he kissed me.

"Ok, no thinking. I guess my most exciting sex fantasy would to be with two men." I said it quick and then hesitated, not knowing how he would respond to that. It could have gone either way. It could have turned him off and made him jealous or mad. Or it could have been a real turn on and he'd push for more details.

"Two men," he said and then hesitated, "any two men in particular?"

"Do you want the truth?" I asked quietly. Unsure if I wanted to tell it and even more unsure if he would be able to hear it without forgetting that this was a fantasy and not reality. I was enjoying this time of quiet playfulness between us and I didn't want to be the one to ruin it.

"Of course I want the truth," he said, "I always want the truth, you know that."

He pulled me closer to him and started to caress between my legs, stroking back and forth like he did when he was in a playful mood. Every few seconds he would kiss my ear then along my neck and shoulder. I started to relax again and told him the truth.

"Well, to be honest, I've had this fantasy about having a menage with you and a close friend of ours. A very close friend of ours." I whispered the last line as he nibbled along my collar bone.

"How close a friend?" he asked, sliding his finger between my labia, he started to stroke my inner lips. "Does this close friend have a name?" he teased.

"Very close. Very, very, close and yes, he has a name." I felt myself getting wet, not only from Brian's playful touch, but from the visual that was occurring in my mind's eye. My fantasy reel started playing in my head. "Our, let's say, partner in crime, is our very good friend, and well...your roommate Paul."

I closed my eyes and waited to see what he would say or do. I'm not sure what I was expecting, but I know I wasn't expecting his next question.

"Really, Paul. Ok," he said lightly and continued with his delicious finger movements. "What exactly are we doing in this threesome, with 'our partner in crime' and my best friend and roommate?"

"Well, we're doing what you do in a menage. We're having sex with each other." I was too nervous to even attempt to try and explain my fantasy.

"I figured that Liv." He slid his fingers out of me and lightly slapped my pussy for my sarcastic answer. It was so unexpected, I yelped and then laughed at myself and him. He continued to ask questions as he slid his fingers back into my warm honeyed sex. "What exactly, in detail, are we doing?"

Brian moved closer to me and held me tight. I stopped thinking about everything I said that morning and realized I was still standing in my entry hall, between two very attractive men, and dressed in nothing but my boyfriend's white shirt. Even though I was half-naked, I felt more exposed emotionally than I did physically. My mind was spinning as I recalled every single word I had said to Brian that morning. I wondered how much of my fantasy he had shared with Paul.

It took a few moments for my head to clear. Brian's grasp tighten on my arms. I looked at him in disbelief. I had told Brian all of the intimate details of my fantasy and now, I was sure he'd shared them with Paul. Looking at Paul standing a few feet away, I knew he was aware of everything I wanted to do with him and Brian.

As I recalled everything I said, I also remembered all of the things I didn't tell him. I didn't tell him my answers to all of my self-analysis regarding why a menage fascinated me. Like, my wanting to see how the power trip felt of being with two men. I didn't mention my need to be wanted by two men, to be used by two men, to be loved by them, or at least, to be lusted for by them.

I didn't tell him, how sometimes I hated the fact that I was always the good girl. I didn't say, on occasion, I wanted to be the bad girl, the naughty girl, even the slutty girl. I'd missed out on all of that in high school and college. I was more focused on doing what was right and focussing on my life's goals. Hell, I missed out on that all my life. I didn't tell him, that this specific fantasy would be like making up for all of, or some of, the things I'd missed out on during my younger days.

I also didn't tell him about the raw feelings, the animalistic feelings I had. About wanting to feel how it would be to be filled by two men, one in the front and one in the back. I didn't discuss how I wanted to feel two cocks inside me as if they were duelling over me. I didn't comment on how I wondered what it would feel like if they banged into each other inside me. I surely didn't tell him that, sometimes, when we were fucking and he stuck his finger in my anus, I fantasized about it being another man's cock.

No, I didn't tell him any of that. I did, however, think about all of the things I told him. Then I thought about the truly intimate, personal analysis I didn't share with him. I did all of this while standing in my entry hall between the two men who were the main characters in my fantasy. I knew immediately that my thoughts registered in my expression.

My face must have gone bright red, because I could feel the heat start in my cheeks and cover my chest. At the same time, butterflies were having a party in my stomach, and my pussy wasn't being left out of the fun and games either. I immediately felt myself become excited and very wet as I remembered the things I said I'd like to do. But, it was a fantasy. Fantasies aren't supposed to come true.

"Are you going to invite our friend and potential 'partner in crime' in or leave him standing in your doorway?" Brian's breath was hot along the side of my face and his hands were sliding up and down my arms, reassuring me, as he spoke.

"Brian, what did you do?" I asked quietly, as I leaned against him to regain the strength back in my legs. I felt as if I was going to hit the floor in sheer embarrassment. All the while, Paul stood in the doorway, smiling and holding two wrapped presents in his hands.

"Happy Birthday, Liv," Paul said, still standing there, looking at me with a hint of concern in his eyes. "It's ok if you don't want me to come in," he said, casually. "I guess this is a bigger surprise than you expected."

He was being so sweet and understanding of the situation. His smile changed from sly to completely kind and caring the second he saw me blush and step back. At first I thought, I hope I haven't hurt his feelings. My second thought was, Don't be stupid, he's your friend, invite him in and figure this out.

"No, Paul. It's fine. Please come in."

I shook my head, a little in disbelief, a little in self-admiration for actually saying it out loud. I thought, Is this fine? Is this what I want? I wondered what I was going to do. Did I just invite my friend in for a drink to be polite, or did I just invite another man into my bed for a menage and a fantasy come true? I wasn't exactly clear on the details at that moment.

"Are you sure?" Paul asked, as if reading my thoughts. He cautiously stepped into the entryway.

"No, to be honest Paul, I'm not sure of much right now. Please come in and give me a few moments to think about all of...this...whatever this is."

"Ok," he said, as he entered and kissed my cheek. "Happy Birthday, Liv." He handed me the gifts. "Don't make any decisions you really don't want to. It's good either way. We're good either way. Understand what I'm saying?"

I nodded and returned his smile and his kiss. How could you not love a guy who was so understanding in the oddest of situations. I felt bad about my reaction. I simply wasn't prepared to see Paul standing there.

I looked from Paul to Brian, then back to Paul. I took a deep breath and focused my attention on Brian. "I'm going to get us some drinks. Then you'd better explain what you were thinking."

Although my words were focused on Brian, my statement was directed to both. I looked at Paul and made sure he knew I wanted to hear from him too. He smiled, held up his hands in an, I'm innocent motion, and nodded his understanding. As I left the two of them and made my way to the kitchen for drinks, I heard Paul's voice.

"Fuck Brian! What were you thinking? She doesn't seem to me like she has any desire to be part of a threesome with me. Hell man, she doesn't look like she wants to be part of a twosome with you right now, my friend."

I smiled as I placed the gifts on the couch table and walked into the kitchen. The first thing I did was take several deep breaths and try to clear my thoughts.

"Oh God, what am I going to do?" The thought ran through my head, but the words came aloud from my mouth. I took three wine glasses and opened a bottle of my favorite red. If nothing else happened, we were going to have some decent wine.

When I left the kitchen, both men were sitting in the living area, quietly talking. Some soft Jazz music played in the background and a few candles were lit. A mood was being set and the two orchestrating it were focused on me. I watched them both, smiling and easily reading their thoughts. Looking from the calm, softer curves of Brian's face, to the more suntanned, weather touched features of Paul's, I realized it wasn't going to be a fair fight. It was definitely two on one, but isn't that exactly the way I wanted it? The naughty thoughts kept running through my brain and I found myself giving in to them.

I couldn't count the number of times I dreamt of having these two men in bed with me. My dreams were so vivid, I'd wake up wondering if I'd orgasmed in my sleep and then question if that was even possible for a woman to do. They were both staring at me. The want and lust apparent on their faces. I laughed to myself as I realized the only things between me and my fantasy coming to life was Brian's white shirt and me saying yes.

"Well, who's first?" I asked, as I placed the tray with the wine and glasses on the table. I had no idea what caused them both to gasp aloud. I looked at two shocked faces and started to laugh. Two men, both over six feet tall, sat there with mouths hung open, practically drooling.

I realized what I said and what they interpreted as my meaning. I laughed so hard; I thought I was going to pee myself. Tears formed in my eyes and I started to cough.

"Don't be so sure of yourselves gentlemen. I don't mean, who's first with me, I mean, who wants to explain first."

I watched as the two men looked at each other, then back to me. Finally, Paul said, "It's your show Bri, you should start."

"Thanks buddy, nice to know you've got my back," Brian said, as he took a sip of wine.

"Don't worry Bri, I'm right behind you." Paul laughed, "A good place to be if Liv starts throwing things."

Brian cleared his throat and started his explanation. "Well baby, the long and short of it is that I wanted to give you something special for your birthday. I wanted to give you something very special, something unique, something you couldn't or wouldn't get for yourself." He took another sip of wine and a deep breath.

"Go on, I'm listening," I said, as I practically drank down my entire glass.

"Well, the more I thought about what that special, unique thing could be, the more my mind kept returning to your telling of a menage between the three of us." He hesitated and looked from me to Paul. "A few days ago, I approached Paul with my idea. I told him about your fantasy and asked if he was agreeable."

"Really?" I looked at the two of them. "So, you thought it was okay to share my private conversation and some of my innermost thoughts with Paul?" I stared at Brian. "And you." I looked from Brian to Paul and asked, "You agreed to participate in a menage without even talking to me about it?"

"Well, a Liv, a..." he hesitated and looked at Brian, "I guess I figured if Bri was telling me about everything, I assumed it was true and that you were open to the idea."

"Do either of you know what a fantasy is?" I waited a few seconds, fully knowing neither would answer my question. "It's something that is in your imagination. It's not supposed to be real, it's like magic and pretense. It doesn't get acted upon.

"You know, make believe, dream like, imagined."

"Does that mean you don't want one?" Brian asked straight out. Now, both sets of male eyes were focused on me once again.

"Liv, you know if you don't want this, all you have to do is tell me and I'm out of here. No harm, no foul." Paul looked at me as if he were more embarrassed than I was. "I'm sorry if you think I was too cocksure of the outcome. I thought it was something you wanted and, well, to be honest, I was honored that you would choose me to join you."

"Oh Christ!" Again, the words that were supposed to stay in my head, came out of my mouth. "It's not that Paul. It's not your fault." I looked at Brian.

"Oh, so I guess that means it's my fault." He tossed his hands in the air like he didn't understand how that could possibly be. "I have to admit, I thought a menage-a-trois sounded a little on the kinky side of sexy. At the same time, I want it, I'm also reluctant." He looked down at his hands, "I'm selfish when it comes to you Olivia. To be completely honest, I'm a little insecure too."

He started to play with his watch band and took a few deep, sighing breaths. "I want to be unselfish Liv. I want to give you the fantasy of your dreams. You've given me so many of mine that I want to fulfill one for you." Brian looked to Paul, speaking to him as much as to me. "Paul is the only person I love enough, respect enough, and trust enough to share you with. He's the only one I'd ever think of giving complete access to you."

"Brian stop for a second. I didn't mean that it was your fault. I didn't even mean you had to explain all of that." I hesitated, trying to figure out what I had meant. "I wasn't questioning your choice in partners, or your reasons. Well, not exactly."

"Well, maybe you could tell us what you mean Liv and what you want. That would make things a little easier and a lot clearer." Brian got up, looking all sexy half naked, and walked over to me as if this whole conversation was normal and could be wrapped up with a simple answer. He kissed my cheek and said, "I thought I was giving you something special, something you wanted, something you would enjoy."

"I need a minute to think," I said. I sat down, closed my eyes, tried to relax, and rubbed my temples with my fingers. I needed to clear my head. My hormones were still on overdrive from screwing around with Brian before Paul interrupted us and it wasn't exactly helping me make a rational decision.

"Here," Brian said. He grabbed one of the presents from the table and handed it to me. "While you are thinking, open this. Hopefully this present will be a little easier for you to accept."

I took it and opened it as I thought about what to say next. It was the camera that I had told him I wanted for my trip when we talked a few weeks ago. Brian paid detailed attention to the things I said whenever we spoke. It was another thing I loved about him. It was another thing I was going to miss.

"I hope it's the right one."

"Yes, it's exactly what I wanted," I said, as I gave him a kiss. "Thank you, baby."

"It's ready to go, camera card and all. Picture ready." He smiled and winked at me. "Hopefully, I haven't screwed everything up. I'd like to make you happy Liv. I tried to make sure everything I did was to fulfill a wish you had shared with me."

"I know Brian, and you did. It's just that the first part could have been handled a little better, I think. Don't you?" Reaching over, I took his hand in mine and watched his reaction to what I had said.

"No," he said, "no, I think it was handled perfectly. It was a surprise, it was what you said you would love to experience at least once in your lifetime. I think you still do, but you're hesitating. All you have to do is say, yes or no." He looked at Paul and as if some silent communication passed between them. Paul got up and came over to us.

"I'm here Liv. I'm here for you, for this if it's still an open option. I'm gone if it's not. It's all up to you." He kissed me softly on the lips and reached down and took my hands in his. Brian was kissing the back of my neck and playing with my hair at my nape.

"It's your choice baby. Yes or no?" Brian whispered as he licked along my shoulder blade.

"Yes or no?" Paul whispered, brought my hands to his lips, and kissed them. Placing my forefinger in his mouth, he sucked on it very suggestively and I felt my body quiver.

I had to make a decision. I had fantasized about this countless times, but did I really want it? Was I making up for what I missed out on in the past or was it something I truly was into doing? My head was spinning with the conflict of the good girl/bad girl thoughts that always kept me from making choices like this.

My fantasies were about hard cocks, maleness, wantonness, and wanting to be consumed by two men. This was different. Here were two real, live human beings. I loved Brian, I really liked Paul. I trusted both of them. Only now, right this moment, did I realize that I wanted both of them. This was my chance to reach out and take what I needed. This was my chance to fulfil my ultimate sexual fantasy.

I decided, this was one opportunity I was not going to pass on. It was like the perfect storm, everything and everyone lined up perfectly. This was a once in a lifetime, never again moment. I decided to take it. Besides, I was leaving town. I could live out my fantasy and escape any potential consequences.

"Oh Christ!" I said, as I took a deep breath and felt my body reacting to these two men. Two men who I knew I loved on some levels, who were my friends, and who I knew would never hurt me. I looked at Paul's big brown eyes staring at me. I felt the warmth of Brian's chest against my back as he pulled me into his arms. My voice was the one I heard break the tension in the room.

"Yes," I said as I looked back at Brian and kissed him. "Yes," I repeated as I turned and gazed into Paul's eyes and squeezed his hands as they held mine.

It was in that moment, that unexpected moment, that my life took a most memorable twist.

~~~~~~~~~~

We walked down the hall as a threesome. Brian leading the way, holding my right hand, and Paul following me, holding my left. All I could think was, Oh God, please let this be as good as I fantasized it would be.

When we entered the room, things seemed to go in slow motion for a while. Paul was in front of me, kissing me lightly on the face and his fingers were tracing along my cheeks and neck. Brian was standing slightly to my right, watching Paul and me as we kissed.

Paul started to unbutton my shirt and I looked to Brian, who gave me a soft smile and took a step back from us to get a better view as I was being undressed by the other man.

Only then did I notice the camera Brian had placed on the bedside table. He'd also brought in the other gift box. I never even saw him pick it up off the table. He tossed it on the bottom of the bed. Then I watched as he slid out of his jeans. He took a few steps back and sat on the side of the bed and unwrapped the parcel. He opening the pink colored box and pulled out my birthday gift.

"Oh Christ."

He'd bought me a Hitachi vibrator, just like that scene in my fantasy that I told him about. "Oh Christ," I repeated as the two men smirked at me, and I felt myself clench my vaginal muscles.

Paul undid the last button on my shirt and placed his hands underneath, gently removing it from my shoulders. He slid it down my arms until it fell from my body, and then looked me over from head to toe. When he returned his gaze to my eyes, he said, "You look beautiful Liv, simply beautiful."

"Thank you," I said. I swallowed the lump in my throat and gave him a quick kiss. caressing my fingers along his cheekbone, over his jaw, and over his chin. I could feel the roughness of his unshaven face; his features were more weathered and sculpted than Brian's. His hands were strong and rough from years of physical work.

While I was still stroking Paul's cheek, I reached back with my opposite hand and touched Brian's smoother, more closely shaven face. I always thought both men were very similar in looks - both tall with thick wavy dark hair and big brown eyes, and both good looking. Yet now, looking at them more closely, more as individuals instead of two friends, they seemed so different from each other.

Brian came to stand behind me, while Paul stepped back and started to strip. He pulled his t-shirt over his head and I was fascinated by the suntan marks along his sleeve and collar line, so different from Brian's even toned skin.

I continued to watch Paul undress as Brian whispered in my ear, "Do you like what you see so far? Taking it all in baby?"

I nodded and nervously licked my lips. Paul undid the button and zipper of his jeans and pulled them off, revealing white boxer briefs. There was something reassuring yet sexy about it, about the way he seemed self-assured even in his white-cotton underwear.

And then he pulled them down, allowing me a first glimpse of his manhood, which was almost fully erect and very thick. I reached back and took Brian's cock in my hand. He too was on his way to a full erection.

Paul stepped closer and placed his hand on my cheek, leaned in and kissed me, more assertively this time. His tongue slid across my lips as he parted them, warm and wet as he entered my mouth, and I soon felt the same. I could hear Brian's breathing increase as my hand stroked over his hard shaft. He reached around from behind me and started to play with my breasts.

He had one soft mound in each hand and he was squeezing and releasing over and over, rubbing his thumbs across my nipples until they were erect and hard. Paul kissed down my neck and over my chest. Brian, guessing his intention, took my right tit, lifted it up and out, and offered it to Paul.

Slowly, Paul brought his mouth down upon the soft tissue. His eyes occasionally peeking up at me as he kissed and licked me. He encircled my areola and began to suckle and tease my nipple with the tip of his tongue. They were both teasing with me, exciting me. Brian cupped one side of me, while Paul played with and suckled the opposite one.

The way they were double-playing me only added fuel to my response, and wetness started seeping from me. Brian lifted and slightly pulled on the breast he had claimed. Paul was now moving between the two, first one, then the other. He'd pull them into his mouth and suck and tongue each nipple until I moaned out loud, repeating this over and over until he got the response he was waiting for.

"Fuck! You two are killing me," I gasped.

I leaned my head back against Brian's chest and my torso arched toward Paul's mouth. Parts of my fantasy were being played out right in front of me and I was having a difficult time believing it was really happening.

Paul made his way from my breasts down to my upper abdomen. Brian gently moved me so that I was standing against the bed, and then murmured for me to sit on the edge. I looked at him, seeking reassurance, and he nodded with a smile. As Paul went to his knees in front of me, Brian's eyes went from brown to black as he moved to sit beside me.

"Lay back and relax baby."

Brian guided me down to a reclined position, and then followed me to the mattress, laying beside me, and we began to kiss slowly and passionately. He was taking my mouth as expertly as ever and tracing my teeth and tongue with his. I was returning his kiss when I felt Paul's hands on my knees, slowly separating my legs.

My moan was quieted by Brian's kiss. His hands were all over my torso, caressing my breasts, my rib cage, and my abdomen. At the same time, Paul had kissed his way up my inner thigh and was now kissing my lady lips. Light, short kisses were placed over my entire sex. Having two men kiss two different places on my body felt totally unreal... Holy Fuck!

Paul's lips were kissing along my wet slit, soft and slow kisses, like little warm raindrops landing on a wet path in the summer heat. His mouth made little kiss noises as he left a trail along my pussy, and when he reached the base, deep between my legs, he started to lick me.

I could feel the flat firm surface of his tongue as he spread me open and licked my inner labia. It was a completely different from the way Brian would do it, using the tip of his tongue in more aggressive movements. Instead, Paul was taking his time as he slowly licked me from back to front with his flattened tongue. He savored the taste and the experience. The sensation was new and unique, and every bit as good as Brian's tried-and-true technique.

Brian's voice sounded quietly, speaking to Paul over my head.

"Don't make her come yet. I want her to come with us both inside of her." He kissed my ear and continued, "That's what you want, isn't it Liv? You want to be teased and tormented a little, but you want to come with us both in you, right?"

My head was foggy, I couldn't find the words, so I simply nodded. Paul stopped licking me and I whined a little as he came up on the bed beside me. The three of us lay side by side.

Turning my head to my right, Brian was there, next to my face. We kissed. Our mouths knew one another; we'd kissed intimately a thousand times. His tongue moved over mine as we teased each other, and I let him lead the way. I loved the way Brian kissed me as if he owned me. It was exciting to feel that control by my man.

Then Paul's warm breath caressed along the side of my neck as he moved closer.

Breaking my kiss from Brian, I turned my head and was met with Paul's mouth waiting for me. His kiss was softer, and he waited for my hesitant tongue to touch his lips before opening his mouth and meeting it with his. Sensing my momentary reservation he slowed the kiss and then withdrew, whispering softly in my ear instead.

"It's okay Liv. There's no rush."

He took my earlobe into his mouth and sucked on it, and then traced my ear folds with his tongue. He blew his warm breath over the wetness in my ear, and I felt a warm wet gush between my legs. Shivers went through me, and goosebumps formed over my skin. Paul chuckled. "You like that, Liv? Good, so we'll keep doing that for a while..."

Allowing myself to get lost in what these two men were doing to me, I sighed and relaxed, at once excited and comforted by their presence and touch.

"Paul's right baby, this is for you." Brian said, as he caressed his hand down the side of my body and rested it on my hip. "Any special requests, Liv baby?"

"I'm not sure..." I said, as I looked from one to the other. Their matching easy smiles reassured me. "I...I think...I'd like to just take things really slowly and maybe just take the time to touch and explore if that's okay."

I felt a little silly saying it. It wasn't like I was a teenager or I hadn't been with Brian a hundred times, but everything felt new again. It felt different. I wanted to savor the feeling. I looked from one set of big brown eyes to the other.

Brian kissed my forehead. "Of course, baby."

"Same here Liv," Paul said quietly, as he played with my hair and moved some tresses away from my face and neck. "Exploring sounds good..."

I smiled, the last of the nervousness leaving me to be replaced with a strong urge to touch them both. I kissed Brian on the cheek, and then turned and kissed Paul on his neck, before turning to a semi-kneeling position between the two so that I could reach both of them. I think they guessed what I was about to do, because they both moved closer to me and turned flat on their backs.

I looked into Brian's eyes and he smiled. Gliding my left hand along his face, down his neck, and across his smooth, almost-hairless chest, I traced his nipples until they peaked into little hard nubs. I pinched them and he sucked in a deep breath and closed his eyes for a few seconds. I could see the pulse in his neck become more visible. Resting my hand over his chest, I could feel his heartbeat- much faster than usual-belying his outward calm. I grinned.

Turning my attention to Paul, I placed my right hand on his forehead and traced along his profile with the tip of my finger. When I drew it over his lips, he playfully bit at my finger and held it between his teeth, winked, and then released it. I caressed his cheek and felt the slightly prickly stubble from the day's growth of beard. I slid my hand over his neck and felt the tight muscles, much more muscular than Brian's, as were his shoulders and arms. Moving to his larger, more sensitive nipples, I played with them, too.

With both of my hands resting over their hearts, I felt their thunderous beat for a minute or so before moving my hands further down their bodies, while my two men kept lying still, heads pillowed on their arms wearing nothing but big, matching grins.

Both abdomens were flat and firm, though Paul's was a little more taut and muscular. I traced their belly buttons and Paul inhaled loudly. Brian's skin flared with goosebumps as my hand caressed further south.

My hands finally reached their goal and I held both of my guy's manhoods in my palms. I slowed my caresses. If it was to be my fantasy, I was going to take advantage of every minute of it. I vividly flashed back to a dream sequence in which I was doing this very thing, and remembered how enjoyable it was to touch and tease both men in my dream world. Reality was so much better. The power in simply holding two cocks in my hands and watching the men's response was intense.

I started to re-enact my fantasy, sliding my hands over their pubic areas. Brian's was virtually free of hair while Paul was all natural. I took in the different sensations in my palms and fingertips.

Stroking and caressing their cocks now, I tried not to be obvious of my internal comparison, but by the knowing grins on their faces I wasn't fooling anyone. I returned their smiles as I took my mental inventory.

Brian's cock was thick and firm. I always thought of it as beautiful, but he hated it when I said that, so I definitely had to remember not to say that with Paul present. Holding him in my hand, my fingers didn't quite meet around him as I started to slowly stroke up and down. His cock grew even harder and I could feel the large vein distend under my caress.

Slowing my strokes on Brian, I started to focus more on Paul. He was fully erect and thick, and I was enjoying the effect I had on him and my view. A shiver of excitement ran down my back as I started to stroke both men more assertively. Their penises pulsated against my palms. Brian's was dark pink, almost purple at his deepest color, and Paul's was a brownish color with a purple head.

I forced my gaze to leave their cocks and return to their faces. Brian watched me intently, but there was strain on his face and he was holding his mouth and jaw in a stiff, tense position. Paul's eyes were closed, as he concentrated on gaining control of his body and his breathing.

Looking into Brian's eyes, I bent and kissed the head of his cock. He gasped as his body tensed.

I placed the same kiss on the head of Paul's shaft. Paul's eyes opened and he watched intently as I kissed him. I heard him gasp, then clear his throat as his cock jumped in my grasp as my lips touched it a second time.

"Sorry Liv, it has a mind of its own sometimes," he whispered lustfully, and stretched his legs to gain a little more control.

I giggled, not minding one bit. Looking from one man's face to the other, debating what to do next, I released Paul's cock from my hold and returned my body and my attention to Brian. I smiled at him and watched as he stuffed a pillow behind his head in order to lift his head a little and improve his view of the activities. He knew exactly what I was planning.

I leaned down and took him in my mouth. I licked him and sucked the tip of his erection, circled the head of his cock with my tongue, and kissed it. I continued to kiss, lick, and suck on him for a minute or two, and then turned my attention and my mouth to Paul.

When I repositioned myself, I saw that Paul was intently watching what I had just done to Brian. He licked his lips and his body tensed as if he were preparing for battle. Instead of going for his penis, though I lifted his balls and began to massage them. His head arched back and his pelvis tilted upward. A-ha! I had found an erogenous zone on him.

Holding one ball in each hand, I took my time massaging each, rolling them between my fingers and caressing them with each hand. With one hand, I pushed him back further as I leaned down and kissed his right ball before taking it into my mouth. Paul moaned as his body tensed, and I repeated the motion with his left testicle, smiling as a drop of pre-cum formed on his cock head.

I lifted my head and looked up at his face, hesitating until he met my eyes, and then licked the pre-cum over his crown. Mmm... I liked his taste a little more than Brian's heavily salted taste. His penis jerked in my hand, but this time I ignored it. I took him into my mouth and slid up and down his shaft until he was in the back of my throat, and swallowed a few times. His voice sounded distressed when he spoke.

"Oh Fuck! Liv, please...don't do that again." He took a deep breath, "I can't hold back on that again." His voice was raspy and full of need. I granted his request and let him slide from my mouth.

Before I had a chance to do anything else, Brian's arms were around me and he pulled me down to the mattress with my back to him and my torso facing Paul. While Paul took a minute to regain his control, Brian was taking advantage of his one-on-one time.

He held my back tightly against his chest and started to move his body in an up and down motion. His erection was level with my ass and kept caressing along my crack. He slid one hand over my tummy and down to my sex, and his fingertips lightly stroked over my pussy and traced my swollen, soft lips.

I practically purred at his touch, wanton and full of need. At the same time I was high on the power of control over these two men. I was completely mind blown.

"Oh Brian, please baby," I whispered, as he kept stroking me with his fingers in front and his cock along my ass.

Paul, now fully recovered, decided he liked the idea of tease play and started to entice me with delicious oral breast torture. He licked, suckled, and nipped at my breasts, his hands caressed them and his fingers pinched at my nipples when he didn't have them in his mouth.

Brian and Paul said something to each other, but I wasn't paying attention to words at the time and missed the exchange. It wasn't long before I figured it out though: my time had come and my men were strategizing on technique.

Paul nodded to whatever Brian had said to him,then moved to the center of the bed and laid on his back. Brian kissed my neck and whispered, "Straddle Paul's waist baby and take him in when you're ready."

Peering over my shoulder at Brian, I caught his soft smile as he nudged me up and toward Paul. Following his touch, I climbed up further on the bed and straddled myself over Paul's upper thighs. Taking a minute to look at him, I drew my hands down his chest, over his abdomen, and stopped when I had his erection in my hands, feeling the heat of his blood as it pulsed through his cock. Looking up to his face, I was amazed by the combination of lust, admiration, and desire there.

I questioned myself for a second, Is this what I want? Do I want to be with these two men? Do I really want to be in a menage? That was the last time I did anything like that. My answer to all of the questions, remained a resounding, Yes. I wanted this. I wanted these two men. I wanted my fantasy to come true.

Sliding up until I was kneeling right above Paul's pelvis, I kept my eyes locked with his as I kept hold of his cock firmly in my hand, loving the feeling of life in it. The warmth, the pulse, the movement it seemed to have even at my slightest touch. I held his gaze for several seconds, suspended above him.

Lifting myself a little higher, I used my left hand to spread my lips open as I slid his penis along my pussy. We both moaned aloud. I was so wet and sensitive, I could see my juices glisten on the tip of his cock. His eyes followed mine to where our bodies were about to meet.

Holding the head of his cock against my opening I slowly lowered myself, inch by inch, onto him. I stretched open to accommodate his girth, feeling my vaginal walls encompass him as he entered me. My vagina molded to his form, holding him tightly inside of me. It was as if Paul was a long lost lover and I was welcoming him home.

Looking into his eyes, I held his cock firmly inside of me. His eyes were deep brown and very clear, as if he could see into my head and knew exactly what I was thinking. I wanted more of a bond with Paul, more than the physical connection of having sex with him. There was a deeper emotional need to know that he was more than my friend. If he truly cared for me, I needed to know it in order to be fully comfortable with what we were about to do. Thankfully, as he moved his hands to hold me and looked into my gaze, he told me everything I needed to know.

When he was fully inside me, I looked at him again. He held his hand, palm open and fingers spread, toward me. Knowing what he was offering, I placed my palm against his and wrapped my fingers between his. His hands were big and his fingers grasped mine. We were connecting physically and emotionally through this simple, but beautiful offering he gave me. I was touched by his sweet, caring gesture.

The fact that he thought to do this for me made me care for him even more. That he wanted to give me that emotional support, as if to say, it was ok, we were ok and nothing was wrong with what we were sharing. Taking his hand, in that moment, was as intimate to me as taking him into my body.

Taking a deep breath, I started to move up and down. Slowly at first, but soon I was overcome with the urge to move faster. Paul must have sensed it because he gently pulled me to him with our linked hands.

His other hand stroked up and down my back. "Let's not hurry this, Liv. Let's take our time to enjoy..."

I slowed my movements to match the caress of his hand on my back, and then felt Brian move behind me, massaging my ass cheeks in the same slow rhythm. As I pushed down on Paul, Brian spread my buttocks open. He placed a kiss on my ass as his tongue started to circle my anus. I gasped and Paul kissed my open mouth and quickly silenced the last part of my moan as my fingers tightened around his grasp.

My body started to tremble as Brian's tongue danced around my dark pink bud like a Whirling Dervish. He knew how that turned me on when he tongued my ass. I was so wet I was leaking around Paul. Then a fleeting thought gave me pause: Christ, he's licking my anus...he knows it excites me more than anything. Does he realize how close his tongue is to his best friends cock?

Fuck. The mental picture of what we looked like from behind was overwhelming. Paul laying on the bed. Me straddling him and taking him inside of me. Brian's face kissing my ass and licking my tight rosebud with his tongue as he held my ass cheeks spread open, darting across my skin so close to his friend's dick...

My muscles tensed, my fingers laced tightly through Paul's. My butt tilted up and back to meet Brian's tongue more fully. I felt my heartbeat race in my chest, my breathing halted for a few seconds, my body shook, and I cried out in the neediest sounding voice I'd ever heard come from me.

"Don't stop. Whatever you two do, don't stop." I gasped.

Brian molded his body against my back, his hands massaging down and over my ass. He continued to caress and tease me while Paul and I started a rhythm of our own.

I felt Brian's hands leave my bottom. I heard the distinct sound of lube being squeezed from a tube. Brian's hands returned, he spread my buttocks and I felt the soft slide of his finger over my anal opening. He drew several small circles over it before I felt his finger enter me slowly. He gently massaged his finger in and out, continuously adding more lube to it as he entered me again.

I wanted to cry out again, wanted to yell, Just fuck me already. It was so easy to give myself to these two men. The sensations that came over me were sheer pleasure. Wonderful, blissful pleasure that crashed over me like a wave.

Even in my wildest fantasy I never imagined how good this would feel. I could see the want on both men and it was the best aphrodisiac ever. I wanted to please them as much as they wanted to please me.

I relaxed my body as Brian's finger entered me deeper and deeper. The pressure was somewhat painful at times, but the erotic sensations it caused were enough to overcome the slight pain and pressure I felt.

I wondered, Is this what it feels like to be the naughty girl, to be a little slutty? Is this what I've been missing all of these years?

Well, at least for tonight, I could do anything I wanted to. I had no one to answer to but myself, my enjoyment, experiencing things with these two men that I never thought possible. I was out of my comfort zone and it was amazing.

Then I felt Brian withdraw his finger, his chest close and warm against my back.

"I'm going to really get you lubed baby. You're going to feel more pressure when I insert two fingers. I need you to relax and bear down when I tell you to. Do you understand what I want you to do?"

I nodded and Brian kissed the side of my head as Paul kissed my neck. I heard the lube being squeezed once more, then the pressure of Brian's fingers on me again. I tried to pull forward, but Paul was holding me firmly against his pelvis. His hands were on my ass and he was spreading my cheeks open for Brian. I looked at him and he tried to calm me.

"Breathe Liv, take a few deep breaths and relax your muscle sphincter." He watched me as I did what he told me to. "Good, now bear down like you're going to go to the bathroom when Brian's fingers push into you." He continued to calmly talk to me as Brian entered me with his middle and forefinger.

The pain increased and I cried out, "Oh God!" Immediately, Brian held still and Paul continued to coax me through the pain. They were both talking to me.

"Relax Liv. It won't hurt as much if your relax your muscle tone," Paul said.

"Nice easy breaths baby, in and out. I'll take it slow. I promise," Brian whispered in my ear as I felt his fingers slowly rotate inside of me. I took a few more breaths before I said anything to either of them.

"It hurts more than I thought it would," I said, holding my eyes tightly closed.

"A little more pressure Liv. I'm going to push in a little more so I know you're well lubricated."

My asshole stretched as the widest part of Brian's fingers entered my tiny hole. The pressure and burn was much more than I ever expected. As I relaxed my tightened muscles, the pressure lessened. The warm lubricant was coating me inside and out as Brian rotated his fingers. My sex gave a little rush of fluid and then heat started to spread through my body.

The warmth from my anus seemed to move towards my sex, then radiated outward and consumed my body. My vagina tightened. I squeezed my ass to hold Brian's fingers in place. Every sensation in my body felt magnified. Reflexively, I started to rock back and forth to take each man into me as much as possible.

Paul felt me tighten around him as my pussy begged to be stimulated. I was never so on fire, so turned on, so fucking needy as I was in that moment. Paul started to thrust forward to meet me. Brian's fingers did the same. My heart pounded in my chest and I wasn't even sure if I was breathing anymore.

Brian's chest rubbed against my back and his thighs were rubbing up against the outside of mine. I knew he was positioned over me as I felt him kiss my ear and whisper to me.

"Are you ready baby? I'm going to take my fingers out." Paul slowed his rhythm as he heard Brian.

I didn't want that. I was finally liking the feeling they were causing in me. "No, don't," I cried out, as my body kept moving back and forth.

"No worries baby, I'm going to give you something else in their place," he laughed lightly before adding, "I'm going to put my cock in you. You want that, don't you?"

"Yes, Oh god, yes!" I cried out quietly. The strain and desire mixed in my voice as I spoke. "Yes, please Brian."

I could feel most of the weight of his body on my back and then I felt the tip of his hard cock rub up against my anal bud. He gently added more pressure and I heard and felt him take in a deep breath.

Wordlessly I answered with a deep sigh and gently pushed back against him. Paul held still, my vagina wrapped tightly around him. The added pressure of Brian's cock preparing to enter my ass was exquisitely torturous. I couldn't stand not having them both inside of me any longer.

My mind was blank. I was in a fog of pure, intense feeling, free of thoughts and words. I was simply sensing our touch, our bodies, absorbing the sense of being connected and soon to be filled by two men. Nothing mattered other than the pure pleasure that was ripping through my body and my mind.

"Do it Brian. Fuck my ass," I moaned between breaths. "I want you both in me. I need to feel you both inside of me."

At first, I felt the pressure of his cock at my opening. Then I slowly felt him push into me. When the crown of his penis was in me, I thought I'd cry out, but I didn't. I breathed through it and made myself aware of every feeling it caused within me. When he stroked my back and entered me a little more, I lost it. I felt the pain, the stretch, the little burn that came with this taboo entry.

"Stop," I cried.

Immediately, both men held still. I took a few deep breaths before I could speak again. "I need a few seconds. It hurts."

"Fuck. Hold steady, Liv" Brian muttered, as he attempted to pull out of me.

I shook my head no, surprised to hear myself say, "No Brian, don't withdraw. Just give me a few seconds to adjust to it." Then I added, "Can you add more lube?"

"Yes. Of course," he said, his voice ridged with need. He applied the warm gel to my opening and around his cock.

He gently pushed in me a little more. As if to distract me, Paul started his rhythmic thrusts as he suckled my breast. I rolled my head from side to side, trying to focus on the sensations

Paul was causing me and less on the burning feeling in my butt. Then the pressure increased as Brian entered me further.

Sensing my tension, Paul slid his fingers to my clit and started to stroke it gently. The added stimulation, of friction, heat, and pleasure was exactly what I needed. Brian entered me fully and I moaned, part in pleasure and part in pain.

At first, their movements were in juxtaposition to each other. Then they started to move in cadence, thrusting their pelvises until they collided with my body. The pressure, the fullness, it was all too much to bear. I started to tremble and shake all over.

Paul slid his hand behind my neck and pulled my mouth to his. His kiss was deep and forceful. He held my head to him with one hand, while his other stroked up and down the side of my body. His tongue was warm and soft as he caressed the inside of my mouth. He licked around my tongue and then licked over my lips with the tip of his tongue. I pulled it back into my mouth and sucked on it.

I heard his muffled groan as I held him tight in my mouth and sucked in a pulsing rhythm on his tongue. I matched his thrusting motions with my sucking action.

Brian growled, "Give it to us-give yourself to us." He pushed into me a little harder, I felt on fire and cried out. "Just let go baby. Enjoy it." he said.

He held my hips in his hands and increased the pace and depth of his thrusts, and soon Paul did, too. His cock slid easily in and out of my sex, the warm, smooth glide of him along my walls in sharp contrast to the hard pressure and overly tight sensation of Brian's thrusts into my backside.

Both were bringing me pleasure. One familiar and the other foreign, forbidden, taboo. It increased my wantonness, pushed me further to the edge.

I was overwhelmed with excitement and pleasure, as if my body was electrified. My senses felt heightened, more alert, making everything seem magnified, intensified. Every nerve and synapse in my body was firing, and I felt more alive than ever before.

Paul's fingers were stroking my clit and then pinched my pink little bud. I bit down on his lip and heard him moan in a combination of pain, lust, and surprise. He pinched tighter and I bucked forward towards him.

Brian's thrusts increased. Paul was meeting him move for move and neither man appeared to be losing stride. I swear they were both banging into each other inside of me. The sensation was so intense, so fucking over the top, that I couldn't hold back any longer.

"I have to come. I have to come now," I gasped into Paul's neck. I buried my face there and held tightly to his arms for support as my body started to shake.

"Let go baby. Let go. Come for us," Brian said from behind me, never breaking his rhythm as he spoke.

Paul reached down and lifted my breast to his mouth. He sucked my nipple and then held it. His suction held such tight pressure that I cried out again, he drew his teeth across my hard nub. Heat shot from my nipple to my pussy; a feeling I had never before experienced to such a heightened degree.

Paul pinched my clit again at that exact moment and I came, releasing hot fluids. My muscles stiffened, my breathing stopped, and my head and back arched. Brian moaned into the back of my neck as my ass tightened around his cock.

"Fuck," he said as he grunted and continued to thrust into my tight ass. "You're so fucking tight around me."

It was too much sensory overload; my system was overwhelmed. I couldn't process anything. So I let go of every thought in my head and allowed my body to feel and to react as it tensed over and over again.

I tighten around Paul as he groaned and came hard deep in my pussy. Spurting warm streams of cum, Paul filled me. Brian continued to thrust a few more times as my anus clenched him tight. A few seconds later he growled again, lightly biting my shoulder as he came.

For an unknown period, it seemed as if time stood still, all three of us were encircled in complete silence, no one moved. Paul bore the brunt of our weight until Brian realized he needed relief.

"Hold on to her and turn Paul," Brian said, indicating Paul's left.

He wrapped his arms around my chest as Paul held my hips and we turned as one, me sandwiched between them, still connected intimately. We lay together on our sides as both men held me securely in their arms.

It was a minute or two before I felt Paul move and withdraw from me, while Brian was still buried deep, so that I could feel his penis move inside every time he adjusted his position. I turned forward a little and I heard him sigh as he pulled back slightly and his cock finally slid out of my anus.

Although they had left my body, I was still surrounded by Paul and Brian, entwined between these two men, and instead of feeling nervous or self-conscious, I felt wanted, safe and protected. Somehow, for some reason, I knew that I belonged there, in the arms of these two men who I knew first as friends, and now as my lovers.

I never felt more happy, more desired, more sated, or more right in my life.

~~~~~~~~~~

A few hours later I woke up. It was late-morning judging by the amount of sunlight coming through my bedroom windows. Free of the limbs that were wrapped around me most of last night, I felt more naked, more than unclothed. I missed their skin against mine. I missed their touch, their smell.

Brian was on his side, his arm was across his eyes, as if to block the light from disturbing his sleep. I loved watching him when he slept.

Paul was on his stomach with both hands crossed under the pillow and hugging it to his face and chest. It was sweet. I pictured he must have held a stuffed animal like that when he was a little boy. Although, I'm almost sure he would have slept in the nude back then. Tempted to slide my hand over his bottom, I resisted, not wanting to take the chance of waking him.

If either of them woke before I snuck out of bed, I doubted I would get very far. I could see Brian's morning erection. I'm sure it would not have taken Paul long to be up to the tasks at hand if he awoke anytime soon. So, I quietly slid to the bottom of the bed and crawled off the end.

Once in the bathroom, I closed the door, and sat on the toilet to pee. The soreness between my legs was a reminder of the previous night. After a long hot shower, I emerged feeling refreshed and clean, but still sore. Tossing on one of my long t-shirts, I pulled my damp hair up into a ponytail and wondered what I'd make for breakfast.

I put the coffee on and started breakfast. Before long I heard noises coming from my bedroom. The two of them were talking and I wasn't sure I liked not knowing what was being said.

Walking to the bedroom, I could hear them through the door. Brian was lying on the bed and Paul was sitting on the side, pulling on his jeans. When I pushed the door open, they looked at me.

"I didn't like waking up without you next to us," Brian said in a tired voice.

I looked at Paul as he gave me a 'me neither' look that made me bite my lip to keep from smiling. I looked back at Brian and winked.

"Well, I had to go pee and make myself pretty for you two." I teased. "I have fresh fruit and bagels for brunch. Hungry?"

"Ravenous," Brian said.

"Then I suggest you get out of bed." I turned and sashayed my hips as I walked back to the kitchen.

"Swing that ass a little more and I'm going to drag you back here woman."

I couldn't help my exaggerate my hip movements a little more and laugh. "Then you will starve." I called back and continued on my way.

"I guess that means, she's not coming back to bed," Paul said.

"I guess not," Brian answered.

"I can hear you," I called back and laughed, "and you're both right."

"So then, that's a definite no." Brian teased, "There's nothing we can do to entice you?"

"You can come to breakfast. That's what you can do." I shook my head as I had the fleeting thought of running back and jumping into bed with them.

A few minutes later, they walked into the kitchen. Both looked so fucking handsome, I couldn't stop myself from staring.

Paul walked over, kissed me good morning, and slid his hand up, cupping my breast. He stroked over my nipple as he pulled me toward him. He winked. The twinkle in his eye said he enjoyed the feel of my breast through the thin material of my t-shirt as much as I enjoyed his touch.

Brian pulled me from Paul's arms, kissed me, then grabbed a handful of ass. His smile told me he liked the fact I wasn't wearing panties. He tried to slide his hand under my t-shirt, but I slapped at it and he stopped.

"Can't blame a guy for trying." He stepped back and kissed my cheek.

We had a nice brunch and relaxed conversation. When we were done eating, they both helped me clean up. Brian asked what my plans were and I answered with the first things that came to my mind.

"I have some shopping to do, laundry, and maybe I'll get some stuff packed today."

I needed time alone to sort through some of the things in my head. I couldn't play with these two all day, even if I really wanted to and, believe me, I did.

"Then I guess we should go now," Brian said, as he started to walk with Paul to the door. "I'll call you later."

"Ok, we'll talk later." I was nervous and had no clue what to say or how to behave when you say goodbye to the two men you just had the best sex of your life with the night before. In a threesome nonetheless.

Hell, I was impressed I made it through brunch without asking a dozen questions. I needed them gone before I said something I wasn't ready to or worse, blurted out something stupid.

Paul wrapped me in his arms, gave me a very nice kiss and said goodbye. Brian waited until Paul opened the door and was half out before he pulled me to him. He kissed me with more passion than his usual goodbye kiss and I wondered if it was because of last night or because of my leaving. Then he gave me a very sneaky looking smile, kissed the tip of my nose, and as he walked out the door he started laughing as he spoke.

"Liv, you should take a look at your camera. I set it up for you yesterday. I'm sure it caught some interesting photos last evening. I had the timer set to take a picture every minute for ninety minutes."

"Brian you did not," I said as he was laughing and walked down the hall.

"Sorry Liv, I didn't know until this morning. I didn't let him look at them." Paul smiled and blew me a kiss. "I thought you should be the first to see them."

"You are so in trouble Brian," I called down the hall as they got into the elevator.

"Love you baby. Enjoy!" he called back and waved.

I couldn't shut the door fast enough. Running into the bedroom, I grabbed my camera from the bedside table, and started scanning the photos. My first thought was, Oh my god! I can't believe this. The more I scanned, the more turned on I became. Not only by the pictures that were captured, but by the memories of everything we did together. I wasn't sure if I should be upset or happy that Brian did this.

I tossed the pillows up against the headboard, lay back, and scanned the pictures a second time. I was thankful the lighting wasn't great, but I have to say, the pics were very interesting and sexy as fuck.

~~~~~~~~~~

As I lay in bed, I thought about the previous evening. Something had changed last night. Something in me had definitely altered. I could feel it. It was more than a physical or sexual change, it ran deeper. I wondered if they felt any different. Was it only something a woman would feel after such an experience? Was it because I had never done anything so wild? Was it because the sex was so different, so exciting?

I mean the sex was good. No, the sex was fantastic. But it wasn't just the sex, or the orgasms. It was the feeling of power I got from having these two strong, handsome, sexy men desire me. It was a powerful, daunting feeling. Surrendering that power to Paul and Brian to do as they wished with me was intoxicating.

What had happened wasn't clear, but I knew it was important. It felt like a life altering moment had occurred. At least for me it had, for them, I wasn't sure.

I felt lighter. My mind didn't feel as closed or as full of meaningless thoughts. It was like a weight was lifted from me. I actually felt like I was relieved of some physical and mental burden. My heart was lighter. My breathing was easier. For weeks now, really months, I had felt like my life wasn't what I wanted it to be. After our night together, I felt like I'd found the answer to most of the questions that had been disturbing me for months.

All the questions I had been asking myself for the last few weeks, didn't seem so unclear now. All of my why's appeared to be less open ended. I couldn't count the number of times I asked myself, Why are you so unsatisfied? What do you want?

I closed my eyes and let these questions run through my head. They didn't seem as unanswerable as they did the last time I asked them.

Had I found something out about myself? Had I found something bigger than me? Was this what I was hoping for, looking for, longing for? Did I need to be part of something bigger than what others had? I shook my head to clear my thoughts and prayed that whatever it was, it would be for the best. I prayed that whatever "it" was, it would come out on the positive side of things for all of us.

The next day, Brian called to see how I was doing. We talked for an hour or two and everything seemed normal between us. It wasn't until a few days later, all of the questions started to come in rapid fire through my brain again.

It had been almost a week since we had been together. Not a day passed that I didn't think about it, see their faces, hear their voices, or feel their touch. It was like my mind was working against my ability to put it all behind us.

I knew it was a one-time thing. It was a fantasy fulfilled. It was a birthday present, a going away present, nothing more. I would almost convince myself of it and then I would talk to one of them or look at the pictures on the camera and my mind was transported right back to that night. I had to do something about this.

The calls from Brian, and then from Paul, weren't helping me to put things in perspective either. I swear they were tag teaming me on the phone. Sometimes one would call, which made me think of the other, and a few minutes later, my phone would ring and it would be the other.

It got to the point that when my phone rang, I automatically waited for it to say, "Call from Brian" or "Call from Paul." I couldn't take it anymore. We had to arrange a get-together and discuss things. Not knowing where we were and how we each wanted to go forward was driving me crazy. The unknown was causing too many questions to form in my head.

An hour later my phone rang. "Call from Paul," was all I needed to hear. My mind was made up. I was inviting them both over for dinner and a chat. I couldn't take this constant state of uncertainty any longer. I never knew what to say to them and it was making things too uncomfortable.

I answered and before he had a chance to even say, hello, I stopped him.

"Hi Paul. Don't talk, just listen. I'm making dinner tonight. I don't care what plans you and Brian may have, but I expect you both to be at my place at seven tonight." I took a deep sighing breath and exhaled loudly. "Make sure you are together and be prepared to talk about things. No excuses, I expect you both here tonight. Any questions?"

There was a few seconds of silence. I thought that I may have wasted my breath and been speaking into a missed connection. Finally, I heard him take a breath and say, "No...Wait, Yes. Should we bring wine?"

I bit my lip so that I wouldn't laugh. He was being polite and asking about wine when I had gone off on him like a crazy lady. I held back the merriment in my voice.

"No. I'll have wine. All you have to do is make sure you are together and on time. That's all I ask. Oh yeah, and be prepared to talk about... where... our friendship stands at present."

"Our friendship?" he said, in a curious tone, almost questioning.

"Yes. Remember, seven o'clock sharp." I hesitated a second to see if he had anything else to say. He didn't, so I ended the call. "Ok, bye."

When I hung up, I took several deep breaths. It was the first time all week that I felt I could breathe easily. My burden was lighter, at least, for now.

~~~~~~~~~~

Dinner was about fifteen minutes away from being ready when the doorbell rang. I swear my heart stopped, for a few seconds, before my legs moved and I was able to walk. Peeking through the security view, I saw my guys standing there. They looked sexy and I was already getting excited seeing them together again.

This evening was not going to be easy. I closed my eyes and made myself a promise. You will not get carried away tonight, there will be no sex, only questions and answers!

Opening the door, I steady my voice, sounding more calm than I was. "Hi guys."

God they looked so good. My pulse started palpating just looking at them. They must have put extra effort into their appearance. Not only did they look sexy but they complimented each other's handsomeness. I had never noticed before how two men could make each other look better but Paul and Brian looked great together.

It was a moment of awkwardness, then Paul hugged me tightly and pulled me into his body. He smelled earthy, very manly, and he kissed me passionately on the lips. He released me and Brian grabbed hold of me. His scent was different but equally masculine. He had one arm around my back and his other hand was cupping my ass. He kissed me.

"Nice to see you Liv," he said huskily.

I guess they didn't listen very well to my instructions. Paul brought two bottles of wine and Brian carried a dessert box. "Come in," I told them, "dinner's almost ready."

Paul opened a bottle and poured us each a glass of wine. "Cheers," Paul said. We touched glasses and each man gave me a peck on the cheek. God, I thought, this is going to be harder than I imagined it would be.

Brian lit candles and dimmed the lights. Paul opened another bottle of wine and we sat down to eat. The mood was starting to get to me. There was an unspoken tension between us. I had been wanton all week and resisted the urge to masturbate. After a night with Paul and Brian my fingers, even my toys, seemed inadequate.

Now here I was with these two incredibly sexy men and my mind was spinning with want and desire. If that wasn't enough sexual tension, I was ovulating. Everything seemed to be in overdrive, including my need for sex. It would be a miracle if I made it through tonight without actually jumping both of them one last time.

I had to start the conversation before I lost it completely. "Guys, I asked you over tonight to talk about last week.

"The sex with the two of you was incredible," I said, hesitating before continuing. "I've never felt so satisfied in all my life. All week long I kept going back to Saturday night. I would look at the pictures on the camera and I would find myself getting excited. At the same time I questioned what we did."

Before speaking again, I looked at them. "Was it right? Was it normal? Do girls like me do the things we did together?"

"Liv, before you go any further," Brian interrupted, "what makes you think we haven't been having similar thoughts and questions?" He hesitated before going on, "Personally I've thought, I'll never do that again because nothing could ever live up to our night together. But then I think, what if..."

Now it was Paul's turn. "Olivia, Brian, I was amazed by what we experienced together. I only imagined sex could be that great." He looked directly at me. "Olivia, I've never seen a woman so radiant and so full of bliss during sex as when we spent the night together. Why do we care what society thinks? And what is 'normal'? The three of us, three people who love each other, care about each other, had a night of mind-blowing sex together. Can that be wrong?

"We enjoy being together and why shouldn't we? I think our bonds to each other are strong enough that if we continued with our present relationship, and the sex thing doesn't work out, although I'm hoping it will, we'll continue to love each other and stay friends." Paul looked thoughtfully at Brian and me. "I say let's see where this goes. What do you two think?"

They had basically just answered all of the questions that I had, but I wasn't about to admit that to them. I was too happy, and too excited to say anything. They both wanted to continue our arrangement and that was all I needed to know.

"I think we should relax, eat the wonderful dinner I've made, drink another glass of wine, and then continue this conversation after dinner," I said nervously, hoping they would be in agreement. As much as I wanted to talk about things and get my questions answered, I needed a little time out before I pulled them both into the bedroom.

"I'm all for that Liv," Brian said and I breathed a sigh of relief. "As long as we pick up the conversation in the bedroom." He leaned over and held my chin so looked directly into his eyes. "Olivia, you're not going to try to tell us that you don't want this to continue are you?" He kissed me. "Because, that would be a lie and we don't lie to each other. Do we?"

Barely able to swallow, I shook my head no and closed my eyes. It was too hard to have Brian so close, talking to me in his sexy, controlled voice, and not want to kiss him. I tried to gather my thoughts and get my feelings down to a simmer, but it was a losing battle. I heard Paul's chair scrape the floor as he pushed back from the table. I sensed his presence directly behind me, before I actually felt him.

His hands were on my shoulders and he was massaging them as he spoke. "I think the dinner will keep for awhile. Do you want to move this into the bedroom right now?"

His voice was sexy, deep, and almost hypnotic. I could hear the desire and tension in his words. It was as clear as the sexual hunger I saw in Brian's eyes. I nodded and scarcely heard my answer.

"Yes." My body was shaking and I couldn't wait to be with them again.

Before I knew it, two sets of hands were on me, lifting me from my chair. In seconds, we were down the hall and in the bedroom. This time they both undressed me, making fast work of it. Brian had my shirt pulled over my head and my bra off in seconds. Paul worked quickly to have me out of my jeans and panties. I was standing in front of the them naked, except for my white socks.

I watched as both sets of eyes roamed over my body and hesitated as they noted my socks were on. One knowing look at each other and they lifted me, placing me on the bed. Each man took a foot and disrobed it. Another knowing, silent glance and they had my feet pulled up to their lips.

Initially, they kissed the top of my feet. Then they kissed each toe. Brian started to suck each toe into his mouth and swirl his tongue around them. It tickled, but it was so erotic, I felt myself become warm all over. I peeked from Brian to Paul. Paul held my gaze as he licked the sole of my foot from heel to toe. He made little circles with his tongue on the arch of my foot. I was definitely turned on by this. I could feel my sex getting wetter by the second.

Both men started to place soft little kisses along the inside of my legs. Their heads bumped when they reached my knees. They looked at each other and smiled. My legs were scissored open as they continued with their path of kisses. Paul was kissing the inside of my thigh and Brian was kissing the outside of my opposite thigh and nipping the flesh of my ass cheek. They worked their way to my center and met at my clean shaven pubic mound.

They took turns with their tongues as they made love to me with their mouths. Brian would kiss along my sex, then Paul would lick my outer lips. Brian would blow tiny breaths over me and Paul would nibble my labia. I watched as one man's head was replaced with the other as they took their turn with me.

I was so overwhelmed by what they were doing and the erotic scene that was taking place before me, I started to tremble. Immediately, I felt four large hands on my body. I was being turned to my side and Brian's hands were caressing all over the front of my body. His hands were large, warm and, except for the hardened skin over his thumbs, soft.

He stroked my neck, my chest, and my breasts. He rubbed over my tummy and my hips. Sliding down my body, his mouth was once again kissing my sex.

Paul's hands were also huge. He had long fingers, longer than Brian's. His hands' were strong, the hands of a man who worked with them daily. I could feel the heat rush to the surface of my skin as they massaged along my shoulders, down my back, and finally over my buttocks.

I pushed back into his hands as Brian started to lick the inside of my sex. I heard Brian groan as he sucked along my inner lips and kissed my clit as I pulled away and cried out in excitement. Paul took advantage of my retreating maneuver and placed his tongue over my anal bud. When I pushed back, I was met with the tip of his warm, wet tongue as it entered me.

Two sets of strong hands grasped me. Paul's hands held my hips and Brian's held me slightly lower on the fleshy part of my ass cheeks. I could feel Paul's fingers grasping into my flesh. Brian was pulling on the fatty curve of my butt, separating my ass for Paul.

I knew what I was in for, and I had no intention of fighting it. I reached down and grasped hold of each head of hair. When I had a full handful of thick, dark locks in both hands, I pulled their heads toward me. Brian in the front this time, Paul in the back.

"Do it!" I growled out the words as I pulled their hair. I heard two deep laughs and then two indistinguishable growls returned. Then I was taken to heaven.

~~~~~~~~~~~~

After they made love to me with their tongues, I took each man one on one. I made love with Brian as Paul watched and whispered in my ear. Occasionally, he would kiss me or stroke me as Brian and I fucked. I no sooner came down from one orgasm with Brian, than Paul was building me into my next one.

When Paul and I were thrusting back and forth, Brian's finger was playing with my ass. Paul plunged into me from the front, and Brian pushed his finger in my backside. The sensation was too much. It was like Brian was trying to touch Paul as he was inside me. The combination of excitement and pleasure as Brian's finger wiggling inside of my ass, Paul's cock slid into my vagina, and the two of them touched inside me was titillating. The thought alone was obscene, yet erotic. I couldn't get the visual out of my mind and I orgasmed hard.

I couldn't hold back any longer, I arched up to met Paul, grabbed his ass and pulled him to me firmly. I bit into his shoulder as I climaxed. I heard him grunt and then I felt his body tense for a few seconds, shake, and collapse on me as he came.

Brian gave a soft chuckle as his hand was trapped under me, and his finger in me, under both of our weight. The last thing I remember was Brian pushing his finger in deeper and Paul's muttered words, as he spoke into the nape of my neck. "Cut it the fuck out Bri. Now."

Brian pulled his finger from me and I laughed quietly as I realized, they could feel each other inside me. It was the last thought I had before my eyes closed. The three of us fell asleep in each other's arms. I don't know how long we napped, but we seemed to awaken within minutes of each other.

~~~~~~~~~~~~~~

We lay there for a while in complete silence, each in our own thoughts. I didn't move and they didn't seem to either. I could feel their bodies encompassing me. It was like being cocooned by two handsome men. I realized I enjoyed the feeling. No, I loved it.

Brian's right arm was under my neck and his left was draped over my chest. His hand was resting, cupped over my right breast. His thumb stroked over my nipple, another habit he'd formed. Paul was in front of me. His head was resting in the bend of his left arm and he was looking directly into my eyes as his right hand rested on my hip and stroked up and down my thigh. Paul was the first to break the silence.

"Are you ok, Liv?" He kissed my forehead and said, "I've been watching how your eyes keep changing and I'm curious to know what you're thinking."

I smiled at him and answered, "I'm good. I'm not sure exactly what I was thinking. I guess I was having random thoughts and not really thinking about anything specific."

"Really?" he said, as his brow went up and his mouth formed a crooked smile. "If I said, I don't believe that, would you give me a more honest answer?"

I've known Paul for almost as long as I've known Brian. Yet, something in the way he often looked at me, made me feel like he saw through my outer defense. My protective wall wasn't as strong with Paul as it was with others. I always thought it was because I was comfortable with him because he was Brian's best friend.

However, as he stared at me and called me out on my white lie, I thought it was more than that. He wasn't looking at me. Paul was looking into me and he was seeing things I wasn't sure I wanted him to see. I wasn't even sure I wanted to see them, but they were there. There was no denying that there were thoughts going on in my head and feelings occurring in my heart that I didn't want to face.

"That's about as honest as you're going to get from me right now," I said and kissed his lips.

"So, you're not denying that you were having other thoughts, you're simply telling me that you're not ready or willing to share them with us. Is that it?" He held my face close to him as he spoke. I didn't think it possible, but his eyebrow shot up even higher.

"I didn't say any such thing Paul, and you know it. Don't put words in my mouth." I looked at him closely and traced my thumb over his lips. My words may have sounded a little harsher than I wanted them to. I was in a good place-we were in a good place-and I didn't want to ruin it.

"Liv, what's wrong?" Brian asked, kissing the back of my head. I felt his chest rub against my back with every breath he took. He pulled himself up next to me until his entire body was spooning against me. He liked the way his penis rested between my butt cheeks when we lay together like this. He didn't know it because I had never told him, but I enjoyed it too.

"Nothings wrong. We're just talking." I reached down and traced the veins in his hand with my finger tips. I loved Brian's hands. I loved how they felt on me.

"She's holding out on us Bri," Paul said. "She's having thoughts and feelings about what happened between us and she won't share them with us."

"Liv, is that true?" Brian asked softly. He rose up onto his elbow and looked down at me. I didn't know what to do or say. Why were they being so inquisitive? Why couldn't they relax quietly or better yet, fall asleep. Although, Brian was never the guy who rolled over after sex and fell asleep. I loved that about him. He would stay up and talk with me for hours after we made love.

I took a deep breath and slowly let it out. I looked to Paul and then up at Brian before answering them both.

"I'm thinking about a lot of things," I said and looked back at Paul. "None of which I'm able to put into words right now and none that I'm willing to discuss with either of you until I think about them and put them in some sense of order and meaning."

"When you do that, will you talk to us about them?" Paul asked.

"Maybe," I answered.

"Why only a 'maybe' Liv? Why not a yes?" Brian questioned. "We've always talked about everything. I don't want that to change."

"Because, if I don't like the answers, or if I don't like the questions, I may not feel comfortable discussing them with you two." I looked from one's eyes to the other's. "That is as truthful as I'm going to get for now."

"Well, then, I guess we'll have to accept that and hope when you figure things out, you also figure out that you can trust both of us with anything you're thinking or feeling," Brian said.

"It's true Liv. I know you trust Brian, but I want you to know that you can trust me too. I'd never do anything to hurt you,"

Paul said, stroking his hand along the side of my face. I placed my hand over his and held it.

"I know that. I know I can trust you both. If I didn't think that was a given, we wouldn't be in this position right now." I winked at him and looked up into Brian's smiling face.

"I like the position we're in baby. I like it very much," he said as he pushed his pelvis forward and held me tightly against him.

"I like it a lot myself," Paul said and kissed my forehead. Then he pulled his body up against mine until every inch of our bodies touched.

The conversation seemed to calm down and we were able to return to a comfortable place again. I felt Brian's hands start to play with my breasts. He was kissing my ear and biting my earlobe, I turned my head toward him. He shifted his body to have a better position as he looked down on me. His eyes were intense, as was his stare. They turned from brown to black and I recognized the signs of arousal in him.

I knew him too well to miss them. First the darkening of his eye color. Then the subtle sexy look he gets as his eyes roam over my body. His nostrils flare a little as he begins to take deeper breaths. It's a very fight or flight animalistic behavior that takes over when he becomes really aroused.

I returned his stare. I felt the heat between our bodies increase. I was hungry for him and that look of his was not lessening my desire. He pinched my nipple between his fingers and I arched my chest upward. His smile was devious. He was playing a game again. I wanted him too much to stop playing now.

"Do you know what I'm thinking about Liv?" he asked in a teasing manner.

"No, I don't." I said, a little cocky, "However, I'm sure you're going to tell me."

Looking into his eyes, I raised my head to kiss him. When our lips met, he took my mouth and gave me a long, warm, deep kiss. As he pulled back, I heard a humming sound come from behind his back. His smile widened as he noted the look on my face. I was blushing. I knew that sound all too well. A second later, I heard the click as he shut the vibrator off.
It didn't take a mind reader. I knew exactly what he was thinking. It had to do with my original fantasy and the use of that Hitachi vibrator. My eyes opened wide and I bit my lip as I returned his gaze. I wanted him to touch me. I wanted him. I

even wanted him to act out my fantasy with me and to use my new birthday gift to do it. But somehow, I knew it wouldn't be that easy.

Feeling the pull of a second set of eyes on me, I turned my head slightly to see Paul smiling at me. His face was a little more difficult for me to read. I didn't know him as well. I did know that he was kind, gentle, and caring. I did know that the look on his face was as hungry as the one on Brian's. I also knew that my feelings for Paul had changed in the past few days.

I was a little confused as to how I could come to care for him so quickly, until I realized one key point. I'd always cared for Paul. I had never realized I could care for him in an intimate way until this past week. Tonight added another level to what I felt for him. I had a slower, calmer feeling of attraction for him. At the same time there was an intensity in our lovemaking that was anything but calm.

Brian's voice pulled me from my thoughts. I refocused on him and what he was saying.

"You know what you have to do Liv. I'm waiting for you," he said, then held the vibrator in front of him and looked over my shoulder toward Paul.

I knew what he was referring to. He wanted me to ask for it. He was waiting for me to ask for him to do things to me. He wanted to hear me tell him and Paul exactly what I wanted. He wanted to hear the words come out of my mouth. Brian wanted to see what a naughty girl I could be. He and Paul wanted to know just how lewd and smutty I wanted to be with them. I had fantasies that were dirty and wanton and I wanted these fantasies to become real. They knew my fantasy and they knew they were a big part of it.

What I didn't understand was how easily these two silently communicated with each other. How they knew what the other was thinking without speaking to each other. They seemed to be able to communicate with a few looks and nods. I wondered how much they had discussed before coming over for dinner. I avoided looking at either of them until I could control the thoughts running through my head.

The last thing I needed was either of them to see what I was thinking. I didn't like the idea of them knowing how much I loved and enjoyed being with both of them, together. I don't know why, but admitting it was more difficult than doing it. I couldn't even convince myself one hundred percent that this whole thing seemed right, felt right.

The silence that came over us now was making me a little apprehensive. I lusted for both these men. By the looks on their faces, they felt the same. I was nervous about what Brian wanted me to say and what they were planning, I actually thought of running to the kitchen and getting us a snack, or a glass of wine, something to break the silent tension I was feeling.

I was about to move from between them and do just that when Brian reached out and touched my leg. I could feel my pulse quicken and my breathing became labored as he held onto my knee. He drew circles around the inside of my knee with the tips of his fingers, and massaged his hand along the inside of my thigh.

My stomach clenched in a knot, my pussy immediately followed. He moved slowly up my thigh, sure of each move he made. The warmth overcame my body and I felt myself giving over to his caress. The nervous tension left my body as I looked into those dark eyes filled with excitement, promise, and most definitely mischief.

"Liv, do you remember what you described to me about this vibe and your fantasy?" he asked in a deep guttural voice.

I remained silent and nodded yes.

I turned as I felt the weight shift on the bed and saw Paul was now kneeling next to me. His pupils were large, almost filling his eyes. Was it lust or determination I saw there? I thought it was mostly desire, but I couldn't be sure. Either way, the energy in the room had become charged. It was like those minutes before a thunderstorm. When the pressure changes, the energy builds, and you can smell the rain in the air. You see the wind pick up and your emotions say "stay" but your mind tells you to take cover.

Only my mind wasn't saying, Take cover. The storm inside me was holding me in place. The pressure was building and needed release. The energy was causing all sorts of mental and physical changes in me. My mind was saying, Tell them what you want. Tell them your fantasy. My body was saying, enjoy the storm and everything it brings with it.

My eyes widened as both men moved closer. Brian's hand was caressing me, at the same time, Paul was lifting me into a kneeling position in front of him. I could see my fantasy being acted out in front of me. My mind became a haze, flashing between fantasy and reality.

"Brian, what are you doing?" I asked, even though I knew exactly what he was putting into motion.

"What do you want us to do?" he whispered as he leaned over my shoulder and kissed my neck. "We'll only do what you ask. Remember our original deal Liv, anything you ask."

I glanced up into Paul's face. His eyes were bearing down on me. His hands were clenched tight and when I looked down, he relaxed them. He moved his glare from me to Brian as he placed his hands on my arms and pulled me a little closer to him.

"Tell us Liv. Ask us for anything and we'll give it to you," he said, with a voice full of lust. It was at that moment that I was sure of the look in his eyes. It was desire, pure sexual desire.

Paul held onto my upper arms while Brian moved up, his fingers brushing along my inner thigh and then reaching my pussy. He glided them lightly over my lips. I was becoming warm and wet again. It was agony not to have him touch me more. My breathing became little audible pants. Other than the sound of our breathing, the room was silent. I swore I could hear our hearts beating.

When his fingers slid between my labia, I couldn't stand it any longer. I lost control and gave in to him. He seemed to always get what he wanted from me. Most often, it was mutually beneficial. In order to get what I wanted from both men, all I had to do was to ask.

"You know you want it Liv. Tell u and it's yours," Paul repeated.

"Tell me baby. Tell us what you need and we'll give it to you," Brian said.

"You know what I want Brian. I've told you my fantasy before; it hasn't changed." I took a deep breath. "Why must I tell you? Why can't you just give it to me?" I was close to begging them to do it already, stop torturing me and fuck me already.

"You've never told me Liv. I've never heard you ask for or describe your fantasy. I've never heard the words from you," Paul whispered in one of the most sexy voices I've ever heard. I felt his breath caress my cheek. I could hear the passion in his voice. It was said as a statement, but I heard it as a plea.

I swallowed what was left of my, not pride exactly, but more like determination not to ask, not to give in. As I thought about it, I realized how silly I was being. I was only depriving myself. I wanted this, they were willing to give it to me, and they needed it for themselves too. I gathered my courage.

"Paul, I want you in my mouth. I'd like to give you head and suck your cock while Brian plays with me, fingers me, fucks me. While Brian uses the vibe on me. I need you to come in my mouth and when you orgasm, Brian will help me to orgasm. I'd love to feel your hot cum shoot into my mouth as I come. Will you give me that?"

"Yes. Yes Liv," he said as he inhaled deeply, "I would love to give that to you." His voice was deep and his eyes were as black as Brian's.

Brian's fingers were still tracing along my sex. Paul leaned down and kissed along the top of my breasts. He took my nipple into his mouth and I felt the warmth from his tongue caress me and merge with the warm feeling that Brian's fingers were causing. It was like the two waves of heat collided and my entire body was on fire.

A low moan came from deep within me and my head fell back and landed on Brian's shoulder. I took a deep breath. The sensation of both of their hands on me, caressing me, taunting and teasing me, was too much to bear. Brian's hand rubbed up my back and his fingers massaged the back of my head. He tangled them in my hair and lightly pulled back, holding my head steady and immobile.

"Ready baby?" he gently asked.

I couldn't form words, so I blinked and bowed my head slightly.

Paul kissed both of my breasts and then knelt back up. Our eyes met and he nodded to me. His hands caressed up my arms and he rested them on my shoulders. He looked into my eyes again and I felt warm all over.

I gave him a slight smile and moved my lips to mouth the word yes.

He looked behind me to Brian and gave one nod. Brian let go of his hold on my hair. He started to massage my back muscles again. Slowly and gently at first, then more firmly. He added pressure until he was pushing me forward and I was pushed down to all fours.

Paul lifted my hair back and held it in a makeshift ponytail in his right hand. I looked up into his eyes and with his free hand, he lifted his cock to my mouth. I licked my lips and made sure my mouth was moist. Then I kissed the head of his cock and took it between my lips. For a moment, I held just the tip in my mouth as I peeked up at him.

I held my breath for a few seconds as I felt Brian's fingers encircle my clit and his tongue lick up the length of my butt crack. I gasped and sucked on the tip of Paul's penis at the same time. I could feel myself moisten and swell in Brian's fingers as Paul swelled in my mouth. The symmetry of the moment was not lost on me.

Both psychological and physical pleasure radiated through my mind and my body. Knowing I caused that response in Paul, gave me great satisfaction. Having both of these men provide me with the same excitement was too much to take in.

I placed my full attention on Paul, trying desperately not to focus on what Brian was doing to me. It was not going to work for long. I took Paul deep into my mouth and stroked him with my tongue. He groaned and placed both of his hands at the sides of my head, still holding my hair in his grasp.

He was holding back. His grasp tightened on my head as he bucked his pelvis forward. I licked the length of his cock and swirled my tongue over him several times. Bucking forward into my mouth a second time, he groaned out my name. I looked up at his face and saw the tension in his expression. He wanted to let loose, yet he was afraid to.

I let him slide from my mouth and heard him groan as he left my warmth. Maintaining eye contact with him, I said, "If you want to fuck my mouth, do it."

I placed his hard cock on my bottom lip and let him rest there while my tongue whipped across the tip of his erection. I pulled him back into my mouth and sucked hard for a few seconds. He closed his eyes and moaned. I could feel his body shake. With one hand I reached up and massaged his ball sac. The muscles in his legs tightened, and he looked down at me confirming he had my permission. I kept him in my mouth, lightly pulled on his testes, and gently nodded.

His grasp on my head tightened and he started to move back and forth, slowly and very carefully at first. At the same time, Brian's fingers entered my slick hole and he was matching Paul's movements. I was being rocked between these two men, and I'd never felt more wicked in my life. I'd also never felt so relished, wanted, and coveted by a man, by two men.

Brian was working his fingers in and out of me easily. Each movement became deeper and deeper. Paul picked up his thrusts and I was barely able to keep up with the feelings that consumed me. I moaned as Brian place the vibe against my clit and turn it on low. At this point, I was so fucking into it, the hum alone threatened to send me over the edge. I held tight and let the feelings of heat, electricity, and pure animal lust fill me.

Paul was thrusting in and out of my mouth, often hitting the back of my throat. I gagged a few times, yet I was enjoying him. We had found our rhythm. Brian plunging and sinking his fingers in me and holding the vibe to my clit. Paul thrusting into my mouth and holding my head, occasionally pulling on my hair. Together, we had found a way to give and receive pleasure as one, and it was fucking amazing.

The scene was playing out exactly as I imagined in my fantasy. I felt free, sexy, and lustful, a little dirty, naughty, and kinky. I also felt wanted, desired, maybe even loved. I knew, I felt safe, protected, and cared for by these two men.

Brian turned the vibe up a speed and I my moan was muffled by Paul's cock. Leaning down, he licked along my ass. His fingers were still inside me and the vibe was wreaking havoc on my overly sensitive clit. I couldn't hold out any longer. I started to suck hard on Paul every time he pushed deep into my mouth. I felt him jerk twice before a warm rush of liquid slid down my throat and he called out my name.

As soon as he had his release into my mouth, I felt a gush of warmth flood my pussy. I was so excited by the control I felt,

Paul's response, and Brian's use of the vibe on me, I was completely overwhelmed. I could feel my juices leak from me. I was amazed by everything we were doing and my body responded.

My pussy was pulsating, my clit throbbed, the warm liquid dripped down the inner side of my thigh. I almost fell to the mattress, but Brian supported me. My nipples were on fire, and I felt like little shocks were being sent from them. When he reached up and pinched one, I rocked forward taking Paul deeper into my throat. He cried out with me.

A few seconds passed before he gently slid from my mouth and lay back on the bed. A moment later, Brian tossed the vibe to the side of us, pulled his fingers from me and flipped me over. I was on my back lying next to Paul, as Brian lay over me. Taking my hands, he interlocked our fingers, and pulled my arms above my head pinning them in place.

He entered me hard and fast, holding his gaze on me. The intensity in which he took me made my breath catch. I turned my head to see Paul reclined back, staring at us with dark eyes. His face calm, his eyes never leaving mine.

I closed my eyes to relax my body and to accommodate Brian's passionate thrusts. I could feel every movement he made inside me. I swore, I was so connected to him, I could feel every bump and vein of his cock. It took a minute or two before he deliberately started to slow his pace. His facial features remained intense, but he was trying to regain his control.

His voice was deep and wanting as he said, "Come with me Liv. I want to feel you come with me, hear you call my name." I swore he emphasized 'my name' when he spoke.

My body tensed and my back arched to meet him. I felt an overwhelming need to give him what he asked for. My entire nervous system was responding to the erotic memories and events that I had just experienced and was still experiencing.

"I want you so bad Liv. I want to come in you. I want feel your pussy spasm around my cock. Come for me baby," he said, as he thrust into me in rhythm with his words. His plea had so much added emotion, that I couldn't help but to respond to him. I released my right hand from his grip and reached for Paul's hand. Paul laced his fingers in mine and Brian laid his hand over ours.

We were connected. The three of us were one again. The thought of these two men and the feeling of being with them pushed me over the cliff. My body tensed, my pelvis lifted toward him. I met Brian's thrusts and squeezed Paul's fingers in my grasp. Sexual pleasure filled me, erotic thoughts of a fantasy fulfilled ran through my mind, and electrical pulses jolted through my body.

I tightened around Brian, milking his cock as he groaned out in pleasure. I couldn't believe I was going to come again, so soon after my last orgasm. I did come and seconds later, Brian followed me. Our bodies strained to meet and we called each other's name.

Brian lay on me as Paul lay to my side. Paul took my hand and held it to his mouth as he kissed it. I looked at him as he mouthed the words, 'I love you' and kissed my hand again. "I love you too," I said aloud. "I love you too, Brian. I love you both."

"I love you Liv," Brian said, "I've always loved you." I'd never heard so much emotion from Brian in all the time I'd known him. He buried his face in the space between my breast and my arm as if he was afraid to look at me.

Lifting up his head, I kissed him softly on the lips. "I know baby." I whispered.

I don't know how much time passed before the three of us fell asleep. Brian on my left, Paul on my right. Brian's arm was draped over my chest and Paul's over my abdomen. It all felt so right.

A few hours later, I woke between two beautiful, sexy men. I went to stretch out and soon realized every muscle in my body ached. It wasn't a painful ache, it was a worked aching. I blinked to clear my vision and looked from one sleeping face to the other. It took a moment before I remembered what we had done a few hours ago. A smiled crossed my face at the memory. I kissed Brian's shoulder, then turned and kissed Paul's.

I barely shifted my weight and I felt two strong arms come across me. One from each side. I held my breath as each man pulled themselves next to me and sandwiched me between them. I had to pee, but I didn't think that was an option at the moment.

I lay there quietly, trying not to disturb my bed partners. I allowed myself to picture what it would be like to wake up like this all the time. To wake up every day, between both of them, would be a fantasy of its own.

Paul moved closer and I turned toward him. Half asleep, he kissed me and asked, "You ok, Liv?"

"Yes. I'm fine. Go back to sleep," I whispered and kissed him back.

"What's wrong?" Brian asked as he nestled up to my back and nudged me until his pelvis was up against my butt and his penis was tucked between my cheeks once again.

"Nothing. Go to sleep." I reached back and took his hand, bringing it to my lips and kissed it.

~~~~~~~~~~

When we woke the next morning, I was more confused than ever. Now, I was really fucking with my own head. I answered one set of questions only to be plagued with a new set. Do I want this? Can we survive a threesome? Is this relationship even doable? And then the two biggest questions that made me want to run. Am I in love with these two men? Can I be in love with two men at the same time?

We agreed to allow twenty-four hours to pass before we saw each other again. I'd talked to both of them on the phone several times, but it wasn't until the next day that Brian asked if I wanted to have dinner with them. I wasn't sure what that invitation included. Did I need to know? Should I ask? Would it be easier to simply go to dinner and let things go as they may?

Dinner was excellent. It came as quite the surprise to find out that both of these handsome men could cook. We ate, we drank, we talked, and we made love. Yes, this time we actually ate dinner in the planned order.

All of my questions were finally answered. For the first time in weeks, my mind was at rest. I was content. I was more than content, I was ecstatic.

~~~~~~~~~~~~

It's a year later now and I'm about to turn thirty-six. These past twelve months give new meaning to the phrase, "What a difference a year makes." It's officially our one year anniversary together.

I never did leave the city or take my cross country trip. I did, however, move out of my apartment and completely change my life. I ended up falling in love. It wasn't your everyday type of love or your typical romance story. I didn't need, nor did I find a Prince Charming.

Brian, Paul, and I worked hard and figured out a way to be together. Instead of a couple, we're a threesome. Instead of the white picket fence, we have a line of trees that surrounds our land and maintains some privacy. Instead of the two point four children, we have two dogs and a few deer and rabbits that feed off our garden in the back.

I never bought or wore the white wedding dress or had the big party. Instead, I found two charming men, who at times, are far from princely, but who I fell in love with and who fell in love with me. I wore a simple champagne colored strapless dress and they both wore black jeans and white dress shirts. The three of us made promises to each other and shared a small intimate dinner in our flower garden.

We need to remember a few things and to keep a few promises to each other. In order to be strong, to work as one unit, and to make this relationship work for each of us, for all three of us, we need to keep those promises we made to each other.

We promised to work together every day to make each other feel happy, satisfied, wanted, and loved. We promised to cherish each other and to protect one another. We promised to be a team and to not allow anyone or anything to come between us. We promised to love and respect each other.

In the end, isn't that what it's all about? Doesn't everyone want to be cherished, protected, loved, and respected by their partner? In our case, we have partners. To me, that simply means twice as much of everything.

~~~~~~~~~~~~~

Brian travels into the city to teach. Paul works in his studio that we relocated to the large barn on the back of our property and I am doing a lot more freelance work. I travel about six times a year for a week or two each time. The goodbyes and the homecomings are spectacular. I'm thinking of taking on more travel assignments so I can have more of the goodbyes and welcome homes.

As I said in the beginning of my story, the main problem with life is it never goes quite the way you expect it to and it absolutely never goes the way you plan it to. The best things about that are, sometimes, it's the unexpected twists and turns that prove to be some of the best times in your life and absolutely, some of the most memorable events.

So here I am. Waking up between two sexy, beautiful, loving men. I've just lived the best year of my life...thus far. I couldn't have had a better year if I had planned it. It's because of that single moment, when I made a decision that changed my life forever.

The moment when I said "Yes!"

...and we continue to live, happily ever after!